Angel of Death . . .

Longarm wanted to go for his pistol but the girl's eyes as well as her bewitching beauty held him fast. The beauty mark just left of her lovely mouth drew to the side. Her hair slid back and forth across her cheeks and her long, almond-shaped eyes were slitted with savage cunning, her lips slightly pooched, her fine, long jaw set hard. The barrel of a rifle poked up from behind her right shoulder, from where it hung down her back by a leather lanyard.

"Who are you?" she said in Spanish-accented English above the shifting of the wind.

Longarm fought against the girl's mesmerizing effect on him, reminding himself who she was, all the deaths she was responsible for. He considered the many more soldiers who would die if she wasn't run to ground.

The lawman hardened his jaw. "The man who's gonna punch your ticket, Señorita!" With that, he heaved himself to his feet and dove forward, his right hand coming down on his Colt .44 at the same time his belly and chest landed on the stony ground. He lifted the revolver. Raising his chin and arching his back to shoot up at a steep angle, he aimed at the clay turret, then promptly eased the tension on his trigger finger.

The girl was gone . . .

DON'T MISS THESE
ALL-ACTION WESTERN SERIES
FROM THE BERKLEY PUBLISHING GROUP

THE GUNSMITH by J. R. Roberts

Clint Adams was a legend among lawmen, outlaws, and ladies. They called him . . . the Gunsmith.

LONGARM by Tabor Evans

The popular long-running series about Deputy U.S. Marshal Custis Long—his life, his loves, his fight for justice.

SLOCUM by Jake Logan

Today's longest-running action Western. John Slocum rides a deadly trail of hot blood and cold steel.

BUSHWHACKERS by B. J. Lanagan

An action-packed series by the creators of Longarm! The rousing adventures of the most brutal gang of cutthroats ever assembled—Quantrill's Raiders.

DIAMONDBACK by Guy Brewer

Dex Yancey is Diamondback, a Southern gentleman turned con man when his brother cheats him out of the family fortune. Ladies love him. Gamblers hate him. But nobody pulls one over on Dex . . .

WILDGUN by Jack Hanson

The blazing adventures of mountain man Will Barlow—from the creators of Longarm!

TEXAS TRACKER by Tom Calhoun

J.T. Law: the most relentless—and dangerous—manhunter in all Texas. Where sheriffs and posses fail, he's the best man to bring in the most vicious outlaws—for a price.

→·← **TABOR EVANS** →·←

LONGARM

AND
SEÑORITA REVENGE

J

JOVE BOOKS, NEW YORK

THE BERKLEY PUBLISHING GROUP
Published by the Penguin Group
Penguin Group (USA) Inc.
375 Hudson Street, New York, New York 10014, USA

USA I Canada I UK I Ireland I Australia I New Zealand I India I South Africa I China

Penguin Books Ltd., Registered Offices: 80 Strand, London WC2R 0RL, England
For more information about the Penguin Group, visit penguin.com.

LONGARM AND SEÑORITA REVENGE

A Jove Book / published by arrangement with the author

Jove Books are published by The Berkley Publishing Group,
JOVE® is a registered trademark of Penguin Group (USA) Inc.
The "J" design is a trademark of Penguin Group (USA) Inc.

For information, address: The Berkley Publishing Group,
a division of Penguin Group (USA) Inc.,
375 Hudson Street, New York, New York 10014.

ISBN: 978-0-515-15309-5

PUBLISHING HISTORY
Jove mass-market edition / June 2013

PRINTED IN THE UNITED STATES OF AMERICA

10 9 8 7 6 5 4 3 2 1

Cover illustration by Milo Sinovcic.

ALWAYS LEARNING   **PEARSON**

Chapter 1

"Careful, now, Sergeant—don't let Señorita Revenge get you."

Captain James Stockley grinned as he reined his Army remount to a halt in the rocky country a few miles north of the Rio Grande in the Big Bend country of Texas, and turned to Sergeant Buff Whitaker. As the big, redheaded, red-bearded sergeant stopped his own horse beside the captain's, Whitaker looked as though he'd been pierced in the ass by a poison-tipped Kiowa arrow.

"Don't worry, Captain," the big man said, stepping gingerly out of his McClellan saddle, and, despite his obvious discomfort, giving Stockley a lusty wink. "If I run into Señorita Revenge out here in these rocks, she's the one in trouble, if you get my meanin'." He stepped back and grabbed his crotch, chuckling lewdly.

As the other men of Company E reined their horses up behind the captain's and the sergeant's mounts, Corporal C. P. Bates chuckled as he regarded the sergeant dipping a hand into one of his saddlebag pouches. "What's the matter, Sarge—feelin' a little heavy in the ole balbriggans, are ya?"

"Musta been that javelina stew he had over at the Toad Creek tavern." said another man, Private Henry Lee, carrying E Company's gold-and-blue guidon, which was buffeted in the hot, dry, West Texas wind. "P.U.!" the corporal squealed, pinching his nose closed. "I can smell that dead hog from here!"

Whitaker pulled out a handful of old newspaper pages and glowered at the eight lower-ranking men sitting their army bays and duns behind him. "You boys keep it up, you'll be on guard duty tonight durin' the dance. And I'll be fuckin' the washergirls from town out behind the dance hall so's you can hear 'em scream!" The big sergeant guffawed, then turned and trudged off through the rocks on the right side of the trail, climbing a gradual grade.

He turned and yelled back, "You soldiers keep your eyes to yourselves. My asshole's shy! Besides, it'll only get you excited."

The redheaded sergeant winked, flashing a toothy grin, and then turned and continued walking up through the rocks. The others watched him, chuckling among themselves. Captain Stockley watched him, too, always grateful for the big man's humor.

Stockley hailed from the green hills of Maryland. Texas—especially the Big Bend country of Texas, where nothing grew but rocks, a few patches of mean-looking cactus, and more rocks—was as foreign and unwelcoming to the captain's Eastern eyes as the moon. Not only was Stockley a long ways from home, but the grade of Indian in this neck of the country was especially depraved—none more so than the mysterious and cunning Señorita Revenge, who'd been killing soldiers in these parts for the better part of four months now.

No one knew why she was on such a feverish rampage against the contingent of the Third Regiment stationed at

Sotol Creek, but a Mexican shopkeeper had dubbed her *Señorita de la Venganza,* or Señorita Revenge, for the Mexicans believed her to be on some sort of vengeance quest.

No one to Stockley's knowledge knew why. Only one soldier had even seen the savage Kiowa girl, from a distance, and lived to tell about it. Some, including Stockley himself, only half-believed the girl was real. He preferred to think the soldiers from the small outpost on Sotol Creek were being taken down, one by one and two by two, by an especially feral *male* war chief leading a dozen or so coyote-like Kiowa braves who were trying to take back the land they considered their own and which encompassed as much acreage as Maryland itself, in and around the Chisos Mountains.

Surely, no girl—not even a savage, dog-eating Kiowa girl—could be capable of such depravity. Maybe the war chief only resembled a girl from a distance? Or screamed like one. Or . . . ?

Captain Stockley was pulled from his reverie by his men's laughter. He glanced at the soldiers behind him, then followed their gazes up the grade to where Sergeant Whitaker was bent forward with his pants around his ankles, flashing his large, round, freckled ass at his fellow cavalrymen.

"I didn't realize there was a full moon tonight, Sarge!" quipped Corporal Bates.

The sergeant gave a grunt, then whipped around quickly and sat down in a nest of rocks, presumably with his large ass overhanging the edge of the rock he was sitting on. The captain couldn't see much of the big man except his head from this angle, and for that the captain, chuckling at the big man's high jinx, was grateful. While the sergeant gave exaggerated grunts and made faces, crumpling up his roughhewn features and crossing his eyes as he entertained the men, Captain Stockley looked around.

They'd seen no Kiowa sign, and for that he was also grateful. He hadn't yet encountered the rabid natives, and while he knew that among the other officers at Sotol Creek he was considered an untested tinhorn, he didn't much care. From what he'd heard, encountering the Kiowa out here in this parched devil's playground, which Stockley privately thought the U.S. government should gladly give back to the rabid aborigines—was usually bloody, and more often than not deadly.

What did white folks want with this country, anyway? Give it back to the savages, if they valued it so highly! Animals were what the Kiowa were. Wild, savage animals.

Being a civilized, educated man with a gentleman's sense of things, Stockley preferred the rolling green hills of his family's sprawling horse farm, where he could freely run his father's Morgans in the rich, knee-high grass of Sussex County, the humid wind from the sea caressing his cheeks, his betrothed, Bethel-Anne de Camp, riding beside him with a wicker picnic basket stocked with roasted chicken, bread, cheese, and wine, her thick, chocolate tresses blowing in the wind.

Nothing around him now but rocks and a breed of cacti called "giant dagger"—a variety of yucca. Per its name, its stems or branches or whatever in hell you called them looked like giant, serrated knives. Christ, what a land this was . . .

Stockley turned to the sergeant still hamming it up for his men, red-faced, growling, puffing out his cheeks as he continued evacuating his bowels. "Sergeant, you're going to need a few more minutes, I take it?"

"Indeed, I am, Captain," Whitaker said. "That old Mexican must have dragged that javelina up out of a dry wash two weeks ago and let it season on his roof. My innards is awfully twisted, I'm afraid."

The other men laughed at the sad clown face Whitaker made.

Tired of the sun and even growing weary of the sergeant's humor, as well as the stench drifting out of the rocks where the big man squatted, Stockley turned to the other men. "Dismount, soldiers. Take a load off. Try to find some shade for your horses . . . if there is such a thing in Texas," the captain added under his breath, looking around wearily, the bright, mid-June sun feeling like a hot knife blade laid against his nose.

Give it back to the damn, rock-worshipping savages who call it home, and send me east of the Mississippi!

Captain Stockley dismounted his own white-socked bay and led the gelding over to a thin slice of shade at the base of a tooth-shaped escarpment jutting a few yards downhill from the trail's left side. The other soldiers dismounted and led their own horses off to similar shade patches a little farther back along the trail, where thumbs of rock reared, giving minimal relief from the blazing, slowly westering sun.

Stockley loosened the saddle's belly strap, then slipped the bit from the mount's teeth. He filled his hat with water from his canteen and set the hat on the ground for the beast to drink from. Leaning back against the relatively cool wall of the escarpment, grateful for the brief reprieve from the sun's forge-like rays on his peeling face, he saw a rider walking his horse along a wash about a quarter mile to the south.

Stockley frowned with concern and started to reach for the army-issue .44 that he wore for the cross-draw on his left hip, but then he saw that the rider wore a tan kepi, yellow neckerchief, and a bib-front blue uniform shirt similar to the captain's own. Stockley also recognized the buck-skin of one of the two scouts he'd sent out earlier, Sergeant Hal Lawson.

The captain had ordered Lawson to rendezvous with the main group along the banks of Hatchet Creek, another couple of miles to the north, just west of the Chisos Mountains. But Lawson must have either cut Indian sign or seen so little Indian sign that he decided that further scouting would be useless.

The mission of Stockley's contingent out here had been to scout along the Comanche Trail, which was being used by several freighting companies hauling freight to and from Chihuahua, and report on Kiowa activity to Major Edward Colby, commander at the Sotol Creek outpost. The contingent had been out here nearly two weeks, however, and they'd seen no sign of trouble along the trail, and damn little Indian sign whatever.

Which had been—and was—just fine with Stockley.

So Lawson had probably spotted the main group taking a break here and decided to ride over to rest his own mount and offer a report.

The man rode slowly, sitting lazily in his saddle, which also told Stockley he had good news to report. If Indians were in the area, he'd likely be galloping, or "fogging the sage," as they said out here, though sage, and green foliage of any kind, was damn sparse in these parts. Lawson kept his head down, likely watching the terrain for dangerous cacti or rattlesnakes.

As the scout continued drifting toward Stockley, the captain turned to regard the other men sitting or standing around with their horses, smoking and sipping brackish water from their canteens. Up the rocky slope, Sergeant Whitaker was still hunkered down in the niche he was using for a privy.

Staring up the slope, Stockley frowned. He walked over to his horse and removed his army-grade field glasses from the padded leather case hanging off his saddle. Adjusting the focus, he stared up the slope until the two spheres of magnified vision became one, and he could see that Whitaker was sitting slumped back in his niche with a red scarf around his neck.

The captain lowered the glasses and stared up the slope with his naked eyes, lines of consternation cutting across his pink, sunburned forehead. Whitaker had been wearing a *yellow* neckerchief, like everyone else in Stockley's contingent.

The captain raised the glasses again, stared through the lenses, and heard himself gasp and jerk back slightly when he saw the half-naked red man crouching atop the boulder to the sergeant's right. The red man's face had three pale lines painted across it, over the bridge of his nose, contrasting the molasses black of his predatory eyes.

In his right fist was a bowie-like knife. Blood dripped from the knife onto the boulder beside the Kiowa's deerskin moccasins.

As the Indian sheathed his knife on his side, and reached behind his back for a bow and arrow, quickly nocking the arrow to the bow, Stockley dropped the field glasses in the dust at his feet.

His first word came out as another, raspier gasp, but then he managed to scream, "*Attack!*" just as the Kiowa atop the boulder near Stockley let his arrow fly.

Chapter 2

The wooden missile sailed down the slope and impaled the back of Corporal Bates, causing the corporal to drop the canteen he'd been drinking from and lurch forward.

Water gushed back out of his mouth. A half second later, Stockley heard the rush of several arrows cutting the air, and he then saw the wooden missiles flying from the bows of a half dozen braves perched on rocks around the group, like phantoms that had materialized out of thin air. Before any of Stockley's group had pulled a gun, the arrows hammered into them—into their backs, necks, chests—with grisly *smacking* sounds.

The men grunted and groaned and did bizarre death dances, reaching for the arrows impaling them. Stockley fumbled his pistol out of its holster and ran forward, heart hammering, screaming, "*Noooo!*" But before he could get a single shot off, what felt like a heavy, oak club hammered into his back.

He took another staggering step forward, dropped his pistol, and fell to his knees. He saw his men falling, screaming, before him. He saw the sun-blasted rocks pitching and swaying around him. He saw the ground directly beneath him shift first left and then right, and then, feeling a searing pain in his back, he reached behind him with his right hand.

He wrapped that hand around the greasy wooden shaft sticking out of him. No, not grease. Blood. It oozed up around the wooden shaft, the stone head of which was embedded deep inside his body, just below his left shoulder blade.

Oh, Christ, it hurt. It felt like he'd been smacked by a lumber dray. His ears rang. The pain spoked from the shaft into all parts of his body, impaling even his balls.

"Savages," he said, as the last of his men fell, sobbing, and their horses galloped away, uncinched buckles clinking. "Oh, you murderous savages!"

Stockley fell on his back. The arrow cracked, driving the head farther into him. He lay there groaning and wheezing, chest rising and falling sharply, digging his spurred, low-heeled cavalry boots into the ground, fighting desperately against the misery. In the field of his vision, Sergeant Lawson appeared, riding up the southern slope.

The man was still riding in that slow, lazy, self-assured way he'd been riding several minutes before, when Stockley had first seen him. The captain propped himself up on one elbow, looked at the soldier riding toward him, vaguely wondering beneath the shock that had addled him why Lawson wasn't reacting to the ambush.

The sergeant's buckskin continued on up the hill and then stopped in front of Stockley, who felt his lower jaw drop when the brim of the scout's tan kepi rose to reveal the oval-shaped, comely, dark-skinned face of a girl. The body straddling the buckskin, clad in the blood-spotted cavalry blues of Lawson, who must lie dead somewhere out in the desert, was at once long, willowy, and curvy.

Full breasts jutted behind Lawson's bib-front uniform shirt.

Dark brown eyes stared out from beneath the scout's tan kepi, pinning the captain where he lay. Footsteps sounded around him, and in the periphery of his vision he saw the Kiowa braves who'd killed his patrol dashing toward him, breath rasping, speaking in their harsh, guttural tongue.

The Mexican girl still straddling the buckskin spoke in the same dissonant language, and the braves stopped suddenly, one pulling back an arrow he'd nocked to his bow and aimed at Stockley. The girl swung down from her saddle and cuffed Lawson's hat off her head. Rich, raven hair tumbled deliciously down around her shoulders. Curling her upper lip devishly, she shook the tresses back and stepped toward Stockley. She unbuttoned the tunic's brass buttons and knelt down in front of the captain.

Her face, with its Indian-flat, tapering cheeks, was the deep red-brown of saddle leather and beautiful, with long, full lips. Just left of her mouth was a small, dark beauty mark. Her chocolate-dark, almond-shaped eyes glowed like sunlit obsidian but with a rapacious intensity, as she pulled the tunic open, her bare breasts jostling only a couple of feet from the captain's face.

They were firm and full, jutting like miniature mountains, the dark-cherry nipples pointing slightly to each side. Despite the terror and misery flooding him, Stockley felt a dull throb of desire. The girl shook her head and grunted, as though to divert his attention from her breasts, and bent toward him, indicating with both her index fingers a tattoo that had been carved into her chest, just above her deep, red-tan cleavage.

The tattoo was in the shape of the Roman numeral 8. Only, as Stockley stared at it, he saw that it wasn't really

a tattoo. A couple shades lighter than her dark skin, it was
a scar, likely carved by a knife that was not overly sharp.
It was about six inches long and as wide as both of the
captain's thumbs.

Stockley lifted his incredulous gaze from the scar to
the girl's eyes that seemed to blaze and throb in their sockets. She drew the shirt closed across her breasts but did
not button it as she rose from her haunches and shouted
orders at the Kiowa warriors who'd formed a shaggy circle
around her and the captain. They appeared to be middle-
aged men and very young men, but their eyes, to a man,
were cunning and feral.

Now I am going to die, the captain thought, a strange
calm washing over him. I'm never going to see the green
hills of home ever again. This parched and barren desert
in which savages dwell will be my eternal resting place.

The warriors closed in on him. While several aimed
their ash bows and arrows at him, two reached down and
hauled him brusquely to his feet. Pain lanced him—so
much overwhelming misery that he must have passed out
for a time.

When he woke, he was being held by two men against
a stone wall, and the señorita was grinning devilishly as
she thrust the point of a knife toward his forehead. Pain
overwhelmed him, and then all went dark, though the pain
never died.

When his eyes opened again, he was riding belly down
across one of his patrol's cavalry remounts. The horse was
trotting, hammering Stockley with wave after wave of
nearly unbearable pain. Dust wafted around him. Blood
dripped from his forehead onto the ground, leaving a trail
of brown droplets curling the brown dust beneath him. His
hands and feet were tied to stirrups. The horse's hooves
hammered the adobe-colored earth beneath him with what

to his tender brain sounded like a hammer on a smithy's anvil.

His forehead burned. He groaned, screamed, wept.

Merciful darkness swept over him again, and in a dream the scar in the shape of an 8 above the savage señorita's red breasts seemed to tattoo itself through his eyes and into his brain.

Chapter 3

A bead of sweat rolled down the lawman's nose as he sat in the rocking coach, staring at the young Mexican girl's breasts jostling behind her cream, fancily embroidered silk blouse. The sweat dripped off his nose and onto his whipcord-clad thigh as the stagecoach careened through the hot, dusty, clay-colored desert of southern Texas.

As if in response to his own perspiration, a sweat bead dribbled down the girl's long, slender, copper-colored throat. It curved a little when it reached her neckline, paused, wobbling a little with the coach's rock and sway. The bead glowed golden in the afternoon sunlight angling into the coach from over Guadalupe Peak far to the west. It winked softly in that soft, late-afternoon light, and then the bead jerked back to life again, and dropped down into the girl's cleavage partly exposed by the open blouse.

Longarm watched it slither down, down into that deep, alluring valley. When it dropped down out of sight between those two round, firm orbs, the nipple of each vaguely outlined against the two or three layers of sweat-damp cloth that tried in vain to conceal it, Longarm heard an anguished groan rise up from deep in his chest.

He saw the girl's full, red lips twitch. When he lifted his eyes to hers, he saw that she'd been watching him, and now, tucking her rich lower lip beneath the rich upper one—causing a small, dark beauty mark near the left corner of her mouth to shift—she slid her gaze out the window beside her, to Longarm's right.

He had the supreme good fortune of riding at the rear of the coach, facing her, on the last leg of his journey to the cavalry outpost on Sotol Creek.

She was about the prettiest thing the deputy United States lawman had seen since entering this baked, devil's playground stretch of Texas, far south of the Panhandle, near the Rio Grande and Old Mexico itself. Had a feeling he could travel nearly anywhere in the world, and she'd still be about the most beautiful thing he or any man could lay eyes on.

She must have had some Indian blood—Apache or Comanche—because her skin was dark, almost the tone of burnished copper. Her face was bewitchingly beautiful—high-cheeked, almond-eyed, smooth-skinned, with a firm, proud chin. The beauty mark complemented the package, sitting as it did just left of her wide, expressive mouth, though at the moment the only thing her mouth seemed to express was a playful, faintly jeering coyness.

Her flashing eyes, nearly as dark as the bottom of a mysterious well, were faintly devilish, telling him she was well aware of the misery she inflicted wherever she went, and especially the near-physical torture with which she was assaulting the tall, dark, weathered gringo clad in a brown frock coat and tobacco-brown Stetson, who sat across from her, facing forward in the rocking, clattering, southwest-heading stage.

As she stared out of the Concord with exaggerated interest, squinting against the roiling dust churned up by the team's hooves and by the heavy, iron-shod wheels, Longarm let his eyes feast on her once more, as though trying to burn this elegantly clad vixen into his brain, so he'd remember her on his deathbed. His gaze traced the outlines of her full, proud, jostling breasts once more, and then, because he felt compelled to utter something, anything, to a young woman he found himself so overwhelmingly attracted to, he said, "Hot day."

He'd said it in Spanish, for he'd picked up a fair working knowledge of the language during past visits to the border. Past *law* visits, that was—for the man, Custis P. Long, was the deputy United States marshal known far and wide by friend and foe as Longarm, and he rode for Chief Marshal Billy Vail out of Denver's First District Court.

She slid her eyes toward him without moving her head, wrinkled the skin above the bridge of her nose, and then continued squinting into the dust wafting up from the coach's wheels. She sucked her lower lip again.

Someone cleared his throat loudly. Longarm turned to the man sitting beside the girl—a Mexican dressed in the outlandishly garish attire of a caballero, complete with wagon wheel, black sombrero, and black bull-hide leggings trimmed with silver conchos. He wore two silver pistols high on his hips, and a big, horn-handled bowie jutted from the well of one of his black, silver-tipped boots.

A man who could have been his dress-alike twin sat beside him. Longarm knew they were the señorita's personal bodyguards, because he'd overheard the trio's conversation when they'd boarded earlier in the little desert town of St. Vincent, twenty miles north of the Rio Grande. Obviously, the señorita was the daughter of an important man, belonging to an important family, and she'd been off visiting for a few days. Now she was on her way home, likely back to a ranch near the little settlement of San Simon and the cavalry outpost nearby on Sotol Creek.

Her regal demeanor and spectacular home-sewn attire attested to that background, as well. So did the eyes of the man who'd cleared his throat in obvious admonishment to Longarm, his gaze hard and menacing. He shifted his eyes quickly to the girl, who'd insisted on sitting by the window so she could see out, while her two bodyguards sat to her right. He jerked those flinty, oil-black eyes back to Longarm.

He was saying silently but none too subtly, "Off limits."

Longarm looked at the girl, who gazed at him sidelong, slightly devilishly, the corners of her fine mouth pulled up slightly. He waved his hand in front of his face, pantomiming, "Hot."

The girl snickered.

She slid her eyes to her two bodyguards, both of whom were glowering at Longarm, then looked at the big lawman again. She winked before returning her gaze to the rocky, dust-veiled desert flying past the coach.

Sitting beside Longarm was a ragged-looking vaquero—a Mexican saddle tramp—in a tattered straw sombrero, with mustaches that drooped six inches past his chin. He shifted uneasily in his seat while the man sitting on his far side—another hombre but this one dressed in peasant's grubby pajamas, under a cracked leather vest, and rope soled sandals—snored with his chin on his chest. His sombrero had fallen off his head to rest in his lap, over his hands.

The Mexican saddle tramp shifted again beside

Longarm, grunted nervously. The señorita's bodyguards apparently made him nervous. He was probably afraid that Longarm intended to make a play for the girl, and that he himself would get caught in the cross fire. Something told Longarm the tramp knew who the girl's family was, and that making any advances toward her, even a purely friendly one, would be a very bad idea.

Longarm sat back in his seat and poked his right hand inside his dusty brown frock coat. Both bodyguards stiffened, hands sliding toward the iron holstered on their hips, their dark eyes boring holes through the big gringo. The lawman froze, grinned, then slowly continued sliding his hand into his coat until he slid it back out again with a three-for-a-nickel cheroot clasped between his thumb and index finger.

He showed the cigar to the two hard-eyed Mexicans. They relaxed, though their faces were set in glowers. Longarm thought that both men had likely been born with colicky scowls. He held the cigar up for the señorita to see, and shrugged questioningly. She merely smiled her rather smoldering smile, not objecting, so he flicked a match to life on his thumbnail and touched the flame to the cheroot, puffing and blowing the smoke out the window to his right. The wind caught it and blew it along with the dust out past the rear luggage boot filled to overflowing with the señorita's accordion bags and steamer trunks.

He took another drag on the cigar. As he blew the smoke out slowly, he frowned, his eyes catching on a man sitting a horse about thirty yards away from the old Comanche Trail that the stagecoach was following. Because of the thick dust and slanting, late-afternoon shadows, he couldn't make out much about the man except that his horse had an Arabian arch in its neck and the man himself wore a sombrero. Cartridge bandoliers were criss-crossed on his chest. He sat there, unmoving as a statue, and then he passed on out of sight behind the rocking coach.

The girl turned to Longarm, lines carved across her otherwise smooth forehead. In the periphery of his vision, he saw the peasant who'd been sleeping on the far side of the stage just then turn his eyes away from the window and sit back in his seat. He kept his sombrero on his lap, one hand under it.

Little lightning forks of apprehension began sparking in Longarm's lower back. He looked out the window once more and saw a tall escarpment moving up fast on the coach's right side. Something moved at the top of the scarp. Longarm saw what appeared to be the end of a rifle barrel a half second before the stage followed the trail so close to the scarp that he could no longer see the top of it.

Something thumped on the coach roof above his head, as though something heavy had landed there. Outside, a man's scream rose beneath the clattering of the stage and the thudding of the six-hitch team's hammering hooves.

The girl across from Longarm gasped.

Longarm's heart leaped into his throat as a rifle's crack reached his ears. A quarter second later, the peasant pulled a big Schofield revolver out of his hat and, cursing shrilly in Spanish, aimed the gun at the vaquero sitting beside the señorita.

The gun thundered. The vaquero jerked back in his seat.

The gun spoke again, and the vaquero sitting to the right of the first one jerked back in his seat with a clipped scream while clumsily raising a Colt conversion revolver from the holster on his right hip. The peasant's Schofield thundered again; in the close confines it sounded like an empty barrel slammed to the ground from high in the air.

The señorita screamed and clamped her hands over her ears. The stage jerked sharply to the left, throwing Longarm hard against the side of the coach. It threw the peasant against the Mexican saddle tramp sitting to Longarm's left, the saddle tramp cursing sharply in Spanish and leaning far back in his seat, as though trying to punch a hole through the wall so he could take refuge in the rear luggage boot.

As Longarm shucked his Colt .44 from its holster positioned for the cross-draw on his left hip, the peasant angled his Schofield toward the screaming man and shot the man in the chest. Longarm aimed across the writhing saddle tramp, who was slapping a hand at the hole in his brisket, and fired once, twice, three times, not allowing the Schofield-wielding peasant to get off another shot.

The peasant dropped his revolver, screaming, and flew back against the door, which opened. He flailed for the side of the door frame to no avail. Screaming, he dropped backward out of the coach and into the dusty wind.

The coach was still moving so fast that Longarm didn't see the man land but only heard the muffled thump of his abrupt meeting with the rocky desert floor on the coach's far side.

The lawman looked around the inside of the carriage, which was moving so fast now that everything was a jouncing blur, the three dead men flopping around madly while the señorita clung to the ceiling straps, wide-eyed, gritting her teeth in horror and against the violence of the coach's breakneck passage down the trail, bouncing off rocks when it skimmed too close to either side.

The door flopped against its frame. The bodyguard who'd been sitting closest to it had fallen to the floor and now bounced on out the door, head and torso dragging the rest of him out and down, leaving his twin to take his place on the carriage floor.

The raggedy-heeled saddle tramp riding to Longarm's left now flopped against the federal lawman, sagging lower and lower in his seat, staring up at Longarm through death-glazed eyes, hatless, his unshaven jaws slack, his mouth forming a near-perfect dark circle between his chapped, pink lips.

Meanwhile, men were shouting in Spanish outside. Hooves thundered. Grabbing the ceiling straps on his side of the coach, Longarm doffed his hat and poked his head out the near window.

A half dozen men in colorful Spanish gear were galloping hell-for-leather behind the stage about sixty yards and obviously trying to catch up. They raked their boots against their horses' flanks and hunkered low in their saddles, some whipping their rein ends, encouraging more speed. Their sombreros flopped behind them from chin thongs.

The lead rider shouted in Spanish to whoever was atop the stage: "Stop the devil's horses, you stupid son of a crazy whore!"

Then he whipped a pistol up and fired. The slug whined inches past Longarm's head, which the federal lawman then drew back inside the coach with a snarled curse. The girl was crouching over the second and sole remaining bodyguard, who'd dropped to his knees on the floor and was slumped over the rear seat as though in prayer. The girl snatched one of his big, pearl-gripped pistols in both her hands and then threw herself back up onto her seat.

Her tan cheeks were mottled pale. Her eyes were dark brown, wide as a bronco mare's who found herself in a field of coiled rattlesnakes. "Marquez's men!" she barked, hardening her jaws. "That stinking depraved son of a horny sow!" she spat out in Spanish most unbecoming a girl of her obvious high station. "If he thinks he's going to *fuck* me, he's going to have to fuck a *corpse!*"

She threw herself to the side of the coach and stuck the big pistol out the window with both hands, shrieking as she fired.

Chapter 4

The girl's gun blasted twice. The wind blew her hair straight forward over her face, so Longarm doubted she even saw what she was shooting at. More pistols popped behind the stage.

Longarm thrust himself forward and pulled the girl back into the coach. "Get in here, señorita," he shouted in English. "You're gonna get your purty head shot off!"

Her brown eyes flung daggers at him. "Unhand me, you gringo son of a bitch!" she said in surprisingly clear English. "Or I'll blow *your* fucking head off!"

She started to raise the big popper in both her slender hands, gritting her teeth as she thumbed the hammer back. Longarm grabbed the gun out of her hands. She screamed savagely. Just as she started to lurch toward him, a bullet thumped into the rear of the stage, over Longarm's left shoulder. It blasted a hole in the front of the coach, over the señorita's right shoulder. She looked at the ragged hole, and her eyes widened in shock. Her cheeks turned paler.

The pistols continued popping behind the stage, hammering two more rounds through the coach's rear wall, flinging wood slivers. One screeched into the wall over the girl's left shoulder, and she gave a yelp and flung her arms over her head. Longarm pulled her down to the floor.

"Stay there!"

She didn't argue but lay flat on the floor that the second bodyguard had vacated when he, too, had tumbled out the flapping door. The saddle tramp now fell on top of her, but she didn't seem to mind having the dead man's protective weight on her.

Longarm wedged her pistol behind his cartridge belt and palmed his own once more, taking a second to gather his thoughts as he spun the double-action .44's cylinder.

The stage was still racing wildly along the trail, bouncing violently off rocks to either side. The Mexicans were still in full pursuit, though they were no longer shooting. Obviously, the team was a runaway, and they wanted to somehow get it stopped, because whoever had dropped onto the stage from the scarp to take command was not doing his job. The team wasn't responding to him. Maybe they'd seen him or heard him shoot the jehu and the shotgun messenger and toss them off the coach and onto the trail, and they'd taken umbrage.

Longarm certainly had. And so had the girl, whom, it seemed, they were after. Having scrutinized her carefully and thoroughly himself, he could understand the compulsion, but the way they were going about it was downright ungentlemanly even for border toughs.

First things first—he had to get rid of the new jehu and get the team under control. He'd deal with the pursuing Mexicans later. As things stood now, the stage itself could roll at any time or be pulled over a cliff, and then, like the girl had said so eloquently, if they intended to fuck her, they'd have to fuck her corpse.

Longarm kicked open the door on his side of the coach. He poked his head out, looked behind.

The Mexicans were about as far back as they'd been the last time he'd checked, their jostling visages obscured by the heavy veil of billowing tan dust. They weren't shooting now, so Longarm holstered his own hogleg. He pressed a shoulder against the inside of the door frame and twisted around, looking up toward the carriage roof.

A brass rail ran along the roof edge. He leaped up and grabbed it with both hands. Grunting and kicking his boots against the side of the carriage, he hoisted himself up above the roof. The carriage lurched violently, and his right hand slipped off the rail.

"Ah, shit!"

Dangling by one hand, he glanced down at the ground racing by, all the little rocks and larger stones casting shadows. Behind him, a gun popped. A bullet clanked off the brass rail near his hand. Another gun popped, and the bullet made what sounded like a baby fart a few inches from his right ear.

The coach lurched again, throwing Longarm back against it, and, grinding the fingers of his left hand into the slippery rail, he threw his right hand over it. He held on, grunting, the corded muscles in his forearms feeling as though they were about to burst the seams in his shirt and coat as he chinned himself up and over the roof.

The man who'd taken the jehu's place was shouting and cursing in Spanish as he stood in the driver's box, the team's ribbons in his hands. He leaned back, pulling on them, jerking on them, to no avail. The team continued lunging forward in its collars, chewing up the trail.

The Mexicans galloping behind the stage were shooting in earnest now, slugs plowing into the roof, spanging

off the brass rail and chewing into the luggage strapped to
the roof, as well. One hammered the wooden back of the
driver's seat, and the tall, rangy Mexican who was trying
to stop the stage glanced over his right shoulder, showing his teeth beneath a ragged mustache, his eyes looking
harried.

He yelled a curse, and then his eyes slid to Longarm. His
lower jaw dropped, and he slid all the reins to his left hand
as he reached for a pistol on his right hip with his right.

Hunkered low on top of the coach, wincing as bullets
chewed into the roof and luggage around him, Longarm
swung his Colt at the driver and fired. The man screamed
and dropped his own pistol as he fell forward and down
the coach's front left corner. The coach lurched up sharply
on that side as first the front and then the rear wheel plowed
over the man.

Longarm saw him again a half second later, rolling
dustily in the trail behind the coach before piling up
against a boulder on the trail's left side. One of the galloping riders' horses kicked him, and the horse lunged forward, dropping to its knees, the rider's shrill scream
drowned by those of his indignant mount.

As that rider disappeared in a dust cloud, the others
kept coming, hunkered low, extending pistols out over their
horses' heads, the pistols flashing, spitting smoke and fire,
the bullets thumping into the stage or screaming around
Longarm's head. He dropped to a knee and returned fire,
throwing two pursuers off their mounts before the others
suddenly hauled back on their own reins, slowing their
horses.

Longarm frowned, incredulous. If he'd discouraged
them—just him and his little .44 and a few lucky shots—
he was going to have to revise his estimation of the border
toughs in this neck of the Big Bend.

He turned his head forward.

If his lower jaw hadn't been so well hinged to his big, leathery, rough-chiseled face, it would have bounced off the coach roof and tumbled into the rocky desert. His heart slowed. He thought it almost stopped as his brain sifted through what his eyes were telling him all too quickly—that the stage had left the trail and taken off cross-country.

Dead ahead, not seventy yards away and closing fast, lay a broad, deep canyon. He could tell by the breadth of the canyon, and by the wide, flat expanse of water stretching out before him, between towering sandstone cliffs, that it was the canyon of the Rio Grande.

Longarm lunged for the reins too quickly. One, they were no longer anywhere he could grab them; two, the stage was rocking too wildly to cover that much ground so quickly; and, three, it wouldn't have mattered if God had handed them to him. He and the girl were going for a swim.

His boots got tangled beneath him, and he fell belly-down on the coach roof. A half second later, as he watched the lip of the canyon sweep toward him, growing larger and larger, his heart caromed into his throat. The team before him was suddenly dancing in the air. For a quarter second he thought they were going to fly, but then they dropped down toward the dark brown water, and the stage began falling after them.

It fell away beneath Longarm, who instinctively kicked out to the side of it, and shouted, "*Hoooolllldddddd onnnnnn, Seeen-yor-eeeeee-taaaaaahhhhhh!*"

Time slowed until seconds became minutes, and he watched the horses and the stage arc downward on his left while he rolled out away from them and found himself sitting in midair, his worn, round-toed boots with their high, mule-eared tops extending out in front of him, his whip-cord trousers tucked into the deep wells.

His gold watch chain floated up from between the flaps
of his brown frock coat, its one end fastened to the battered, old turnip in his left vest pocket while its other end
was attached to the double-barreled derringer in his right
vest pocket.

He watched his hat fly out of the stage and sail in the
air to his left, close enough for him to grab if he'd had a
mind to. And then the stage door sprang open and out and
the saddle tramp rolled out, as well. He was followed, with
a shrill scream, by the señorita, her long black hair blowing nearly straight up above her head in the wind.

As she plummeted beside Longarm, the wind lifted her
gold-embroidered red vest, shirtwaist, and camisole,
exposing her full, tan, uptilted breasts with firm, dark pink
nipples.

Even in his dire predicament, plunging toward the gap-
ing Rio Grande, Longarm couldn't help marveling at the
perfection of the señorita's bosoms and thinking that they
were even more spectacular than he'd previously imagined,
when he'd been ogling them in that halcyon time only a
few minutes ago—though now it seemed like days—just
before the peasant drilled lead into the señorita's bodyguards, the stage became a runaway, and Longarm's death
became imminent.

He looked down at the river growing before him, below
his boots, filling his vision and blotting out the sandstone
cliffs on either side. A white waterbird screeched at the
objects plunging toward it, and squawked raucously as it
took flight, its wings beating white ruffles on the otherwise
calm surface of the Rio Grande, which Longarm slammed
into so hard that he was momentarily knocked senseless.

Senseless, that is, except for a feeling of cold envelop-
ing him and the screeching of a thousand indignant angels
in his ears. The screeching was interrupted by a deep

thudding sound, and then a large, invisible hand threw him to his right, rolling as he plunged down, down into the muddy waters of the river. Vaguely, as his senses returned after the hammering concussion, he realized that the thud had been made by the stage and the horses crashing into the water to his left.

He held his breath but heard himself groaning against the bubbles rising from his nose. He'd taken only half a breath before the river had snatched him out of the air, and he felt as though his head and chest would explode from oxygen deprivation. In his ears, his heart sounded like a sledgehammer beating a gong every half second or so.

His boots touched the soft, sandy bottom. He ground a heel into it, used it to propel himself upward, flinging his arms above his head, swimming desperately for the surface that hovered above him like a pale blue sheet seen through isinglass.

He shoved his head through the wavering skin, opening his mouth wide to draw a deep breath that thundered through him, quelling the hammering of his heart and the throbbing in his brain. He looked around, saw some roiling bubbles and small whirlpools where he assumed the horses and the stage had plunged beneath the river's surface, the horses having all likely been killed by the impact with the water. They were too heavy to have survived the violent plunge.

The señorita?

Longarm swung his head around, treading water. A body floated behind him, near the middle of the river. He recognized the saddle tramp floating facedown, his face to the sky, limbs akimbo, rising and falling in the gradually settling waves kicked up by the crash.

There was no sign of the girl.

Longarm drew a deep breath and dove beneath the

river's surface once more. He swam beneath the dead man, toward the stage that was a large, dark-red-and-yellow box rolling slowly onto one side, the unmoving horses streaming out in front if it, all dead, as Longarm had suspected.

He returned to the surface, drew another breath, dove again. He looked around frantically before he saw a long, oblong object floating about midway between the surface and the bottom. He swam for it, grabbed the girl, hauled her to the surface. When he had her head out of the water, he turned her onto her back and, one arm hooked over her chest, began swimming furiously toward the near shore, the same side of the river from which the stage had plunged— the U.S. side.

The shelving shore touched his boot toes. He ground his heels into it, straightening, lifting the girl in his arms. She didn't move. He didn't think she was breathing. When he got to the gravelly shore, he laid her onto her belly and wasted no time in placing his hands on her back, and pushing.

"Come on, girl," he said, breathless, water sluicing off of him. "Let's get that river out of you. Go ahead—*cough!*"

After pumping her back hard several times, he felt her begin to wriggle around beneath him. She convulsed, lifting her head, and water gushed out of her mouth and onto the gravel.

"Once more," he said, pushing on her back one more time.

The girl grunted, groaned, and, gagged, turning onto her rump, bending her knees, breathing hard, and looking at him. "That's enough. Thank you." Her English was nearly perfect. Her breasts, strikingly revealed by the wet shirtwaist and the camisole beneath it, rose and fell sharply as she breathed, wheezing, turning her head to one side to continue clearing her lungs.

Longarm turned away from her, ashamed for ogling her at such a time but even more ashamed for the warmth of desire her comely form had evoked in him. He sat back on his butt, glancing out at where the stage and the horses had sunk. He shook his head, clearing the shock out of it.

Then, remembering the Mexicans who'd been chasing them, he heaved himself to his feet. His soaked boots squawking on the gravel, he moved toward the cliff while scrutinizing the crest, a couple of hundred feet above, with his eyes, shading the westering sun with his right hand. He moved his hand to his cross-draw holster, pleasantly surprised to find the .44 still snugged down in the soggy sheath.

"Marquez, you said?" Longarm asked the girl, his eyes detecting no movement on the top of the cliff.

"*Sí,*" the girl said, lying back on the gravel, her natural cherry tone returning to her cheeks now that her lungs were cleared. Even looking like a drowned river rat, with her raven hair pasted against her head, her fancy clothes clinging to her, she was still beautiful. "Marquez." She curled her upper lip and wrinkled her nose.

"Friend of yours, I take it?"

"No," she said, shaking her head, not catching the irony in his tone. "No friend of mine. An *enemy* of mine. An enemy of my *father's*! Banditos from the other side of the border!"

"Must be gone now," Longarm said, returning his gaze to the top of the ridge, moving around as he scrutinized it carefully. "Good thing, too . . ." He palmed his Colt, inspecting the soaked weapon, wondering if the cartridges would fire. "My Winchester went down with the coach." Since the stage had been so crowded, he'd stowed the prized long gun in the rear luggage boot, though even if he had it now, he doubted it would fire until he'd cleaned it and loaded it with fresh, dry shells.

A gun popped to his right. Automatically, he spun, crouching and extending the Colt.

Riders galloped toward him and the girl from downstream, along the canyon bottom. There must have been a good dozen or so. Smoke puffed from the pistols they triggered skyward in warning.

Chapter 5

Longarm looked around for cover. He saw a nest of boulders that had probably fallen from the ridge crest. "Come on!" he urged, reaching for the girl's arm as the riders continued hammering toward him, triggering shots.

She jerked her arm out of his hand as she stared toward the approaching riders. "Father!"

She hauled herself to her feet and ran toward the horsebackers clattering toward her along the rocky, sandy shoreline. The lead rider, a gray-haired, well-dressed man in a ten-gallon Stetson, holding a Winchester carbine and straddling a black Thoroughbread, reined up abruptly.

"Valencia!"

"Father!"

As the gray-haired, gray-mustached man, who appeared Anglo to Longarm, swung down from the Thoroughbred's back, most of the other riders checked their own mounts down—all except two. These two, both gringos, galloped toward Longarm, aiming rifles at him, the lead one shouting, "Drop the pistol or take a bullet, mister!"

Not wanting to be shot over a simple misunderstanding,

Longarm quickly tossed the Colt into a sand pile and raised
his hands, palms out. "Don't get your neck up, friend," he
said, "I'm . . ."

He ducked as the lead rider, in a funnel-brimmed hat
and with hard, pale blue eyes, swung the butt of his rifle
at him. Longarm had ducked a hair too late, and the rifle's
butt plate glanced painfully across his temple. Enraged,
he lurched forward, grabbed the arm holding the rifle, and
pulled the man out of the saddle.

The man gave a clipped cry as he landed hard on the
rocky ground, the rifle clattering down beside him. The
other rider was still galloping toward Longarm, grinning,
intending a similar maneuver as the first man, with the
butt of his Henry rifle.

Longarm ducked that blow completely, hearing the
wind rush of the brass-plated butt swinging over his head,
and then rammed his head and shoulders against the side
of the man's coyote dun. The horse lost its footing on the
slippery stones, whinnied shrilly, and went down hard on
its rider, who yelped as the horse pinned his left leg to the
rocky shoreline.

"You son of a bitch!" bellowed the blue-eyed man,
scrambling on hands and knees for his rifle, his pugnacious
face brick-red with fury.

"Kelsey!" This from the gray-haired man standing with
the girl, who was facing him, gazing up at him beseech-
ingly. "Kelsey, let him go!"

Kelsey froze with his hand on the carbine. He left the
gun on the ground but swung his scrunched-up face at
Longarm. "Why the hell should I?"

"Because I said so," said the señorita's, gray-haired,
gray-mustached gringo father. "Because Valencia says this
man saved her life." He slid his gaze toward Longarm now.
"She says he's not with Marquez."

"That's right," Longarm said. "I don't even know Marquez. But I'd like to remedy that!"

The gray-haired man's mouth quirked up. He turned to his daughter, took her arms in his hands again, shook her gently. "You're sure you're all right?"

"*Sí, sí*," she said. "I am all right. I almost drowned, but"—she glanced over her shoulder at Longarm, her eyes cast with gratefulness—"I'm all right now. Philippe and Gabriel are both dead. Marquez had a man dressed as a peasant aboard the stage."

The gray-haired man nodded. "Figures." He removed his corduroy coat, wrapped it around the girl's shoulders, then walked toward Longarm. He was a medium-tall, slender man, probably in his late forties, early fifties. Weathered and sun-beaten, his brown eyes shrewd, cunning, suspicious, he stopped before Longarm, obviously sizing the big lawman up, before extending his hand.

"Sam Quine."

Longarm shook the man's hand. "Custis Long, deputy U.S. marshal out of Denver."

The man frowned, puzzled.

Longarm said, "I'm here on business. Just happened to be aboard the stage, headed for the Sotol Creek cavalry outpost when that Marquez man filled your daughter's bodyguards with lead."

"I'm glad you were here, Marshal." Quine glanced at the second man who'd attacked Longarm and got his horse thrown on top of him for his trouble, and who was just now getting to his feet, as was his horse. "I do apologize for my men's actions. I hope you weren't too badly hurt."

Longarm swiped at the blood dribbling down from the cut on his temple. "I'll live."

"My men and I had gotten word the stage bringing my daughter back home might be attacked by Marquez, a common border thug who'd hold her for ransom, so we rode out to meet it." Sam Quine sighed, shook his head. "Just in time to see it go over that cliff. Hope I never have to live through a start like that again. Doubt the old ticker could take it."

He stuck out his hand again, and his men started to remount. "Anyway, Marshal, I'd love to stay and chat, but it'll be dark soon, and I suppose you heard this country is being threatened by a wild band of Kiowa. I'd like to see my daughter safely back to Three Forks before night descends."

He turned and spoke to one of the men sitting his horse near where Valencia stood, shivering and staring toward her father and Longarm. "Ren, hop down and give the marshal your horse. Leave the saddlebags and the saddle-ring carbine in its sheath. He'll need the gear to get him to the outpost."

He turned back to the soaked lawman still dripping water onto the rocks around him. "It's the least I can do."

Ren leaped off a long-legged grullo mustang, with a blaze face and white spots across its hindquarters, and hopped up onto the back of another rider's zebra dun.

Longarm said, "Normally, I wouldn't take payment for what needed doing, but since I seem to be without any other means of transportation . . . and defense . . . I'll take you up on your offer, Mr. Quine."

"Please, Sam." Quine smiled. It didn't appear to be an expression he was used to making. He had the look of a hard-bit Texas frontiersman about him, one who was aging but certainly not softening. Vaguely, Longarm wondered how such a man had come to have a Mexican daughter with obviously a good dose of Indian blood. If she was a product of his own loins, nothing in her appearance betrayed the fact. His wife would be a rare beauty.

Quine walked back to the girl. The two men who'd attacked Longarm, the one limping badly and cursing under his breath, swung back into their saddles, casting hard, predatory looks at the man who'd roughed them up.

Ignoring them, he said to Quine, "Would you throw some directions to the outpost in with the horse?" He glanced around at the sandstone cliffs sheathing the broad river that was turning purple now as the sun fell. "I reckon the detour from the main trail might have gotten me lost."

Quine helped his daughter up onto his saddle with a grunt. "Take the same trail up the ridge we do. Ride straight north until you come to another trail. Take it west. You'll run right into San Simon and the outpost on the other side of it." He took the Thoroughbred's reins in his hands and walked around to the horse's left side. "You wouldn't be here about the Kiowa, would you?"

"I would at that."

"Had a feeling." Quine swung onto the Thoroughbred's back, behind his daughter, who kept her eyes on Longarm as she crouched forward, chilled. "Those men out there aren't much good at trackin'. I hope you are."

"I hope so, too."

"That Señorita Revenge," Quine said gravely. "She'll give you fits."

Longarm scowled. "Señorita Revenge?"

This was the first he'd heard the name. All he'd learned from Chief Marshal Billy Vail, who'd sent him down here, was that his mission was to track a small but especially wild and sneaky pack of Kiowa who for the past several months had been not only killing soldiers willy-nilly, but also robbing army payroll parties and privately owned stagecoaches hauling the U.S. mail. They slipped back and forth across the Mexican border at random, making them

very difficult for the U.S. Cavalry company stationed at
Sotol Creek to deal with.

"That's right—Señorita Revenge," said Quine. "That's
who leads them savages. A savage herself, feral as a rabid
coyote. Probably no older than Valencia here. She's made
a laughing stock out of all of us, especially them soldiers
over to Sotol Creek."

Several of the other men snickered.

"Anyway," Quine said, leaning forward and lowering
his head to plant a kiss on his daughter's cheek, "thanks
again, Marshal. Good luck hunting that demon Injun gal.
I got a feelin' you're gonna need it!"

The man turned his horse and rode away with the girl,
who cast one last, quick, beguiling glance at her benefac-
tor, lifting the corners of her mouth ever so slightly. The
other riders fell into line behind their boss, the two Longarm had dusted looking back at him with malevolent
stares.

Longarm checked over the grullo to see what kind of a
mount he'd been given, stopping short of looking the gift
horse in the mouth, however. Deeming the horse sound,
he unsaddled it and hobbled it near where he decided to
build a camp for the night and dry himself out before continuing on to the Sotol Creek outpost.

When he'd finished tending the horse, he gathered dry
driftwood, kindling, and tinder from along the quietly lapping waters of the Rio Grande. Shivering as the sun fell,
the canyon angling dark shadows out from its walls, chill-
ing his still-sodden body, he arranged the tinder and kindling in a ring of stones, and, using matches he'd found in
the grullo's saddlebags, started a fire.

Standing near the warming flames, he kicked out of his
boots, emptied the water out of each, and undressed down

to his birthday suit. The loss of his prized Winchester haunted him. Deciding he couldn't get much colder, he walked into the river and dove down to the stage now lying on its side at the bottom, about fifteen feet below. There was just enough light in the middle of the canyon to separate the coach from the murk. He had to surface three times for air before he'd finally retrieved from the rear luggage boot not only the prized weapon in its soft leather sheath, but his saddlebags, as well. He dragged the gear back to the surface and carried it to shore.

He spent the night drying himself, his saddlebags, and his clothes out by the fire, and taking his Winchester apart and cleaning each part carefully with an oily rag from the grullo's gear. The gear also consisted of a small, flat bottle half-filled with brandy, a small bag of Arbuckle's, and a pouch of jerky. His own supplies, of course, were soaked. Working on the gun, he sipped coffee he'd brewed in his own pot, laced with brandy, and chewed the jerky—a sparse meal but a welcome one after all he'd been through.

"Thanks for this latest assignment, Billy," he muttered as if he could tell his boss, Chief Marshal Billy Vail of Colorado's First District Federal Court, who was probably now safely ensconced behind his supper table in Denver, not far from the bustling Larimer Avenue. "Sure do appreciate it. Not only do you send me to southern Texas, the asshole of the planet, but you send me there in the middle of another sweltering Texas summer. Before I even get to my destination and start my assignment, I get hoorawed by some crazy Mex named Marquez out to fuck some gringo's purty Mexican daughter—though I have to say I can certainly understand the urge . . ." He chuckled wryly at this as he ran the rag through the Winchester's trigger guard, scouring out the mud and debris that had fowled the trigger.

He continued muttering while the flames cracked and popped and the coffeepot gurgled softly. "Marquez takes over the stage, and the team runs off like their tails are on fire and dump me and the gorgeous little señorita in the fucking Rio Grande! I bring the purty little Mex girl back to life—Valencia was her name," he said, smiling and saying the name again just to hear how it sounded—"*Val-en-cia!* Only to have her father's men try to drill me third and fourth eyes I couldn't see out of even with glasses."

Longarm sighed. "Thanks a bunch, Billy!"

He sipped the coffee laced with brandy, yearned for a cigar. He looked around, saw the cheroots in a soggy brown clump near his saddlebags. They looked like a small pile of fresh dog shit. "And to top it all off, all my three-for-a-nickel cheroots are soaked to the gills!"

He finished the coffee, then went out and evacuated his bladder in the river. He discovered his hat a ways downstream, where the river had washed it ashore. Returning to the fire, wearing only his damp hat, he found most of his possibles dry, so he combined his own gear, including cooking utensils and spare clothes, with a few bits of chosen gear from the ranch supplies, into one set of saddlebags. Then, finding his clothes sufficiently dry, he dressed, spread out his blanket roll, added one more stick of driftwood to the fire's dwindling flames, and lay back against his saddle, drawing the blankets up to his chin.

One thing about south Texas summers—at least the nights were cool. Too cool, in fact, after a river swim. The stars flashed over the canyon, reflected in the Rio Grande's stygian waters that continued lapping quietly, lullingly. A couple of coyotes yammered in the distance.

There was a slightly louder sound—a splashing sound. Longarm sat up in his blankets and reached for his holstered Colt as he turned to the river. He froze, leaving the gun in its holster.

Valencia stood at the edge of the shore, in the starlight, brown and naked, river water streaming off her like liquid silver.

Chapter 6

"You're one purty señorita, Miss Valencia."

She walked toward him, tan and glistening, her black hair flowing wetly down her strong but slender shoulders, touching her proud, firm, uptilted, brown breasts that jostled slightly as she moved. She stepped lightly, gracefully, her bare feet making no sound on the gravel. She knelt down beside him, reached under the blankets, and wrapped her hand around his hard cock.

The organ grew harder as she squeezed it, flexing her hand around it gently.

"Longarm," she said in a sexy-breathy whisper, "I wanted to make love with you from the very first minute I laid eyes on you in the stage."

"Gotta admit," he croaked, "I sorta had the same notion myself."

He drew her to him, pressed his mouth to hers. Her lips opened for him. She groaned deliciously, and the groans grew as they kissed, sword-fighting their tongues. Hers tasted faintly like brandied cherries.

At the same time, she stroked his cock gently, her hand feeling like warm, slick silk around him.

He lowered his head to the valley between her breasts, drew deep of the sweet-musky smell of her, then licked the right one while he ran the nipple of the other gently between his thumb and index finger, feeling it come alive. She groaned, tipped her head back, pumped him harder.

When he'd slathered each nipple until it fairly throbbed in its pool of saliva, he lay back in his blankets and drew her up onto him. She gave an eager little grunt as she straddled him, leaned forward, her hair brushing his chest, and reached between them for his cock. Very slowly, holding it up and steady in her fist, she slid her wet pussy down over the swollen head.

"Oh!" she said, lifting her chin and gritting her teeth.

She lowered herself still more, until she was thoroughly impaled and grinding around on him, the head of his cock feeling to Longarm as though it were jammed somewhere up around her belly button. He could feel her wet womb expanding and contracting around it as she began sliding up and down on him, pressing her knees up close against his sides.

While she fucked him, he alternated kneading her breasts and sucking them and sliding his hands down and behind her to caress her round ass as it rose and fell on top of him.

She groaned, sighed, and cursed in Spanish, until she was bobbing in a frenzy of jostling black hair, between the wings of which her face was a mask of blissful misery and almost unendurable torture. The beauty mark on the left side of her mouth was as dark as her hair against her cherry-tan face. Their bellies slapped together madly.

Longarm groaned as he felt himself galloping up perilously close to the broad, deep canyon of his passion.

When she came, she arched her back and threw her head back on her shoulders, quivering as though she'd been lightning struck. Longarm let himself go then, too, grinding his teeth and curling his toes and then reaching up to squeeze each of her delectable orbs again, feeling them shake along with the rest of her as he bucked up against her oozing snatch.

Their spasms dwindled in unison.

Slowly, she lowered her head, released a long, relieved breath, then crouched to press her sweaty breasts against his chest, her lips to his. She let her tongue dance around in his mouth for a time, and then she gave his lip a playful nibble, and straightened. She winced as she rose, his cock reluctant to slide out of her. And then she stepped out away from him, coquettishly chewing the nail of her right index finger, and walked out toward the dark river flashing in the starlight.

"Where you going?" he asked.

"Home."

Nibbling her finger, she glanced back over her shoulder at him, smiling bewitchingly between the tussled wings of her rich hair. And then she stepped into the water and waded outward, the dark river slowly climbing her long, slender, brown legs. It inched up to her round, tan buttocks and then rose to cover them.

When she was up to her shoulders in the water, she turned back to him, smiling. Only it wasn't her face that was smiling, but a red devil's face, long, green fangs pulsating as she threw her head back and laughed. It was a shrill scream like that of a thousand demons suddenly released from hell. The scream echoed around the canyon as the black water continued rising until it had consumed her and there were only a few small waves to mark her passing.

Longarm lifted his head from his saddle with a startled grunt, looking around wildly, heart hammering. Breath raked in and out of his lungs. He turned to the river.

Nothing there but darkness. His fire had burned down to a few, scattered orange coals.

"What the hell?" he said, glancing back behind him. "Valencia?"

No response except the distant shriek of a hunting bobcat and the quiet, soothing lapping of the river against the gravelly shore.

He shoved a hand down inside his blankets, grabbed his crotch, felt the wetness there. He slammed his head down against the saddle. "Shit!"

Still feeling a little depleted as well as disappointed by the wet dream, he woke at dawn and built up his fire for coffee. When he'd had a couple of strong cups, and several hunks of jerky, he rigged up the grullo and swung into the leather. His spare carbine hung by its saddle ring; his freshly cleaned, oiled, and loaded Winchester '73 was snugged down in its scabbard.

He rocked around on the Texas-style saddle that sported a big, silver-trimmed horn. He preferred his lighter, Cavalry-issue McClellan, because it was easier on a horse's back for long, hard rides, making the animal more efficient, but he'd left the McClellan back in Denver. The trip down here to the Texas boot heel was too long and laborious to be lugging that much gear around. He was just happy to have his rifle and saddlebags, with his spare shirt and underwear and cooking supplies.

In the pearl wash of the dawn, he followed the trail that Quine and his men had taken out of the canyon. It switchbacked twice, gradually, giving him plenty of time to reflect on his dream of last night, until he had to suppress the start of another hard-on. He shook his head—such dreams were bullies to shake—and put his mind to the task at hand, which, namely, was finding this far-flung cavalry outpost at Sotol Creek, which seemed to be right smack-dab in the heart of the current Kiowa trouble.

When the grullo gamely crested the cliff, Longarm let it have a blow while he looked around at this vast country that now, as the sun edged above the horizon, resembled a vast corduroy quilt stretched across a floor strewn with objects of all shapes and sizes. The sun's vibrant, angling shine added a lemony tinge, jutting shadows westward of bluffs, hills, mesas, boulders, and the many varieties of cactus and sparse sage plants that were about all that grew here.

He found the stage road and followed it north between shelving mesa walls, the ratcheting shrieks of a hunting eagle following him, echoing off the steep cliffs surrounding him. A rattlesnake coiled in the shade of a century plant, giving the grullo a start, but the rattler did not strike. It was probably too hot to strike, Longarm wryly thought.

He met a couple of freight wagons manned by Mexicans, their wary expressions and handy rifles and revolvers bespeaking the latest Indian threat. He met a freight wagon driven by two men in cavalry blues, the insignias on their arms indicating a corporal and a sergeant. Longarm pinched his hat brim to the men as they passed, but they each barely nodded in return. Glancing back through the wagon's dust, he saw a third soldier hunkered in the rear, beneath the cotton canvas. He was manning the menacing steel mosquito of a Gatling gun.

They were likely hauling or retrieving supplies from another town or outpost, and they were bound and determined to not be harassed by the Kiowa. And by Señorita Revenge . . .

Longarm mulled the name and what Quine had told
him about the girl, wondering how the band of kill-happy
Kiowa had come to be led by a woman. A young one, at
that. He was eager to find out more at the Sotol Creek
outpost.

Late morning, as the sun hammered down brightly,
blasting its furnace-like heat, Longarm rode up over a jog
of hills bristling with cacti. A town rose around him—a
haphazardly arranged collection of mud-brick and plank-
board shacks sporting viga poles and brush roofs, mostly
looking badly dilapidated and sun-faded. Some had out-
door ovens in their yards. Stock pens flanked the shacks.
Chickens pecked in the trail while several goats grazed
the spiky, yellow grass growing along its edges.

A little, round-faced Mexican boy, maybe three years
old, sat on a low, barren hill along the trail's right side, singing softly and poking at the ground with an ironwood stick.
He was naked save for a pair of ragged deerskin shorts.
Longarm waved to the boy as he passed, and the boy stared
at him, singing and continuing to play with his stick.

Longarm continued along the trail that wound through
a crease in the hills, until the hills flattened out somewhat
and he approached what appeared to be the heart of the
town, which a board sign along the road, propped against
a sprawling mesquite, had identified as San Simon. Here,
the buildings along both sides of the trail were more con-
centrated, some only slightly larger than the shacks he'd
seen earlier—business buildings, they were, some with
Anglo names, like Johnson's Drygoods or Percival C. Han-
dly's Theraputants and All-Natural Elixirs, though there
were many more with Mexican names, or with no identi-
fying names at all, attesting to the fact that Americans
were fairly new to the region.

White adobes hunkered in the unforgiving sun, with

chickens strutting around them, children playing, Mexican men in straw sombreros and white pajamas hoeing small, irrigated gardens or dozing in slender bits of shade. Women of all shapes and sizes toiled about their yards, grinding grain or hanging up or taking down wash or beating hemp rugs with sticks. Some of the men held demijohns of wine, possibly pulque, on their thighs, and either smiled ethereally or dozen drunkenly.

Longarm hadn't ridden much farther before he recognized the "border element" here—a mix of Anglos, black men, Mexicans, Indians, and sundry combinations thereof milling about the cantinas and saloons and whorehouses or casually riding into or out of town. Mostly, they were unshaven, dressed in ratty garb, wild-eyed, and armed for bear.

Longarm knew he could set off a powder keg in any cantina and probably eliminate three or four names from federal wanted rosters. As he passed one little adobe hovel with a rusty, corrugated tin roof, he could hear what sounded like French being spoken loudly within—an angry man's voice.

As he continued on past, he spied movement against the building's north wall—a big, fat soldier with long, greasy black hair putting the wood to a Mexican girl bent forward across a rain barrel. Her skirt was bunched around her waist, and her naked brown breasts raked against the rain barrel, causing her to curse through gritted teeth, as the big man, with a private's stripes on his blue uniform shirt, hammered against her from behind, wheezing.

Longarm stopped the grullo and turned it toward the fornicators. He frowned, poked his hat back slightly, and tipped his head to one side. The big man stopped pumping against the whore and turned his head toward Longarm, scowling, his greasy hair hanging in his eyes.

"What the hell are you starin' at?" His voice had slowed considerably near the end of the question, so that "starin' " and "at" had been separated by a full two seconds. His little, deep-set eyes narrowed further, and his lower jaw loosened.

"*Darryl?*" Longarm said. "Darryl 'the Dog' Luther St. Vincent, sometimes known simply as 'Dog' or, ludicrously, '*St. Vince*'?"

The man stared. His jaw hung a little looser. Then recognition flashed in his dark eyes, and he bellowed, "*Longarm!*"

He snapped his right hand up behind his shoulder. Sunlight flashed off the steel blade in his fist. Welcome to San Simon, Longarm vaguely thought . . .

Chapter 7

Longarm's right hand snaked across his belly, filled with three pounds of Colt, and barked loudly once and then a second time. There seemed to be so much tallow over St. Vince's heart that the first bullet only stunned him. When he tried throwing the knife again, which he'd had sheathed behind his neck and under his shirt, Longarm fed him the second half ounce of lead.

He didn't want the whore to get cut with a careless swipe of the killer's knife.

St. Vince stumbled backward, tripped over his pants that were bunched around his ankles, and fell on his back with a fart and a grunt. The whore screamed and crouched behind the barrel, eyeing Longarm cautiously, apparently expecting him to shoot her, too.

He raised the Colt's barrel and told her in Spanish, "Don't worry, señorita. I have nothing against you. Only that dog there."

He cursed as he swung down from the grullo's back, irritated at having to waste his time on the man. He'd have ignored him and ridden on if he hadn't been on the lookout

for the man for several years, ever since he'd killed a sher-
iff's deputy and judge from Laramie. Longarm had
doubted he'd ever run into him again to clear the paper up
on him. Now holding his pistol out in front of him, Longarm looked around to see how the other folks in the area
were reacting to the killing.

There wasn't much reaction at all. At least, no one
appeared to take offense. A few people glanced toward
him, a couple of drinkers even stared, but no one came
forward. They all merely continued with their business,
as though killings were as common as bowel movements
in this neck of the frontier.

Turning back to the dead man, Longarm saw the whore
shove her skirt down and then lift the straps up over her
arms, covering her breasts, as she scrambled over to the
dead man. She dropped to her knees, gave Longarm a pro-
prietary glance, like a coyote with a fresh meal in sight, and
then started rummaging around in the man's pockets.

Longarm snorted. He'd intended on hauling St. Vince
to the Sotol Creek outpost, where he'd likely been stationed, hiding from the law behind his cavalry blues, but
he decided to let the commander send someone for him
later. Let the whore pick his carcass clean. She likely
deserved it.

Longarm swung back into the saddle, gave a parting
glance at the girl. She was kneeling with a small pile of
coins and a couple of greenbacks on the ground near her
bare foot while she inspected the blade of the knife that
St. Vince had tried to use on Longarm, appraising its value
or possibly its usefulness. He booted the grullo on up the
street, scattering a small flock of chickens and incurring
the wrath of a small yellow dog that appeared to have some
coyote blood.

Ahead, two American soldiers in sweat-stained cavalry

blues were walking toward him, along the right side of the street. One of the men wore a palm-leaf sombrero. A wad of chew bulged his cheek. Sweat stains ran down from the armpits of his blue, bib-front tunic nearly to his black cartridge belt.

The two soldiers stopped when they saw Longarm, who, in his snuff-brown hat, brown tweed coat, and brown whipcord trousers stuffed down inside his mule-eared cavalry boots, stuck out in this border town like a cheap whore at a Lutheran wedding dance.

"That you doin' the shootin', mister?" asked the man in the palm-leaf sombrero. He wore a sergeant's badly frayed chevrons on his shirtsleeves. The other man was taller, with long blond hair limp and dark with sweat, and he had a gold spike in his ear that Longarm doubted was regulation.

"That's right. One of your men. Darryl 'the Dog' Luther St. Vincent, also known as St. Vince."

They looked at each other, and then the one in the palm-leaf sombrero said, "You must mean Sergeant Willie Vincent."

"No doubt," Longarm said with a caustic snort.

"Who the fuck are you, amigo?"

"Deputy United States Marshal Custis Long out of Denver. I'm on my way to the outpost on Sotol Creek to see a Major Colby. The stiff yonder is a known killer and fugitive from federal justice, and I blew his wick when he pulled a knife on me. You'll find him three doors down with his dick facing heaven."

"Marshal Long, did you say?" said the taller of the two. "The major's waitin' for you. Look for a sign that says 'Colby's Jail.' Just up the street. That's where you'll find him."

Longarm started away. The one with the long, blond

hair said, "Just so's you know, the major don't allow the discharge of firearms in his town."

Longarm frowned. *His* town?

"When I see him, I'll beg his forgiveness," the lawman said. "That'll be my first order of business." He pinched his hat brim and gave an ironic grin.

A few minutes later, he saw the sign COLBY'S JAILHOUSE protruding out from the front of a small, stone building with a brush-roofed front veranda and bars over its deep-set windows. The stone building was old, the chinking between the stones crumbling and missing altogether in places. The sign, however, looked new—clear black letters set against a crisp white background. The sign was supported by two ironwood poles, and it extended out from the far side of the porch, nearly high enough above the ground for a horseback rider to pass under.

A straight-backed, silver-haired gent in a dark blue cavalry tunic stood on the porch, smoking a meerschaum pipe carved in the shape of an eagle, the head being the bowl, the wings extending to either side. The leonine-headed old gent with a major's brass crossed-sword insignia on the front of his blue kepi looked like he could have stepped off any Civil War battlefield. His bearing, right down to his frosty blue eyes, bespoke old cavalry. So did the nasty scar extending across his left eye and angling over the middle of his nose. There was a nick out of the nub of his opposite cheek. An old battle scar, knotted, twisted, and paled with time.

The major watched Longarm obliquely as the lawman pulled the grullo up to the hitch rack fronting the jailhouse. The lawman looked at the sign, puzzled, and then turned to the older man, who was obviously waiting for him to speak. "Well, Major, I see you're open for business."

The man had been standing just outside the jailhouse's

open door. Now he moved slowly forward and knocked the dottle from his pipe on the porch rail. "Long?"

"Major Colby?"

"Been expectin' you."

"Well, I'm here. And no sooner had I ridden into town than I shot one of your men fucking a whore back yonder, outside a homey-lookin' little cantina."

"Shot him?" Plucking a small pouch from his coat pocket, the old major scowled at Longarm. "I don't have enough men left out here for you to ride into town shootin' 'em. You're supposed to be savin' 'em, not killin' em."

"He was a wanted man, but he didn't seem to *want* to come willingly, though I offered . . ."

The major sighed and shook his head in disgust as he dipped the meerschaum's bowl into the tobacco pouch. "I hope you're not going to blame me for that. I know it's the fort commander's duty to check his rosters against that of government wanted lists, but I haven't received one of those lists in a month of Sundays. And even if I did, most of those fellas change their names. Besides, I need every able-bodied man I can get. I only have about thirty or so left out here, and Fort Stockton doesn't have enough to spare."

Longarm swung down from his saddle. He led the grullo into the shade cast by the large sign and slipped the bit from the horse's teeth. He unbuckled the latigo strap so it could breathe easy. There was a half-filled water trough near the hitch rack, though Longarm held the horse back from it, wanting it to cool down first. He'd found it to be a good horse, and he didn't want to ruin it.

Keeping an arm hooked around the horse's long, fine snout, he glanced at the sign once more, then returned his gaze to the major now puffing his meerschaum to life, the flame of his lucifer dancing before his weathered, bearded, hollow-jawed mug and badly scarred nose.

"What's this about, Major? You're takin' over the law here in San Simon?"

"Early last winter, yes. Had to. Desperadoes rode in and shot the town marshal and his three deputies. Then they hanged 'em out along the banks of Sotol Creek, south of my outpost yonder. I woke in the morning to a fierce howling, and looked out the window of my quarters to see gray desert wolves tugging on the hanged men's feet, trying to pull the bodies down."

Major Colby flicked the match into the dirt near Longarm's boots and exhaled a long plume of fragrant pipe smoke through his nostrils. "The town marshal was a former soldier—Captain Everette Green. Piss-burned me, them curly wolves ridin' in here like that tryin' to show they could do whatever the hell they damn well pleased. When I couldn't find another good man to take over the law duties, I decided to do it myself.

"I'm the law in the town now. Town Marshal slash Major Devlin Colby. I assign a different half dozen or so deputies to make the rounds every week. Oh, I know it's not regulation, but out here, long since forgotten at regimental headquarters, you might as well throw the regulation book out the fucking window or be dragged down by the wolves that haunt this region."

He narrowed an eye at Longarm—a crazy eye, Longarm saw now. He'd seen such eyes before, way out on the backside of the wild and woolly frontier. "I'm talking wolves of both the four-legged as well as human variety. Not to mention the dark-skinned savages that keep running amok."

Longarm studied the man. He didn't have to study him long, however. He knew what kind of craziness men existing this far off the beaten path could be driven to. Hell, an outpost commander taking over the law of a town might not even be all that crazy, if no one else wanted the job.

Anyway, that wasn't what Longarm was here for.

"Tell me about this Señorita Revenge," he said, releasing the grullo's snout so the horse could dip its head in the trough. "Since that's what I came all the way down here for."

"Hold on, Marshal." The major was staring off to the west, past the scraggly edge of the town and toward the collection of adobe brick buildings that hunkered amid the rocks and cactus on the far side of what Longarm assumed was Sotol Creek. Among the crude shacks, an American flag was buffeted by the dry breeze.

A rider was coming along the well-worn trail between the outpost and the town. A female rider in men's rough riding attire, though the curvy body and billowing yellow hair told Longarm the rider was all woman. She rode lightly in the saddle, breasts jouncing around behind the light blue blouse she wore with form-fitting denims, a matching blue ribbon in her hair. This girl did not ride sidesaddle, and she appeared to wear stockmen's boots with spurs.

A wicker basket hung down from her saddle horn, a red-checked oilcloth tucked neatly over it.

Longarm watched the girl trot into the town, and the vast sky arching over her and the outpost and the great copper hump of the Chisos Mountains rising behind, made a romantic backdrop to the beautiful blonde's entrance. The town itself was less than quixotic, but the contrast only favored the girl, Longarm saw, as she waved and smiled, showing white teeth between ruby lips.

"Hello, Father—I hope you're hungry!"

Her voice was soft and fairly chiming with girlish innocence. As she reined her black Morgan horse up beside

Longarm's scruffier looking grullo, she glanced at him, and their eyes held.

Her smooth, youthful, lightly tanned cheeks were touched with crimson, and then her eyes sparkled as she shyly glanced away.

Chapter 8

"I could eat two horses," said Major Colby, smiling down at the girl. "As you can see, Clara, we have a visitor. The deputy U.S. marshal I was telling you about. Custis Long, please meet my daughter, Clara Colby. She lives with me out at the fort. Keeps my life from falling into complete disarray."

"Well, I try my best," the girl said in a high, sweet voice.

She tempered the sweetness of her voice and the innocence of her eyes, however, when she swung her right, black, white-stitched boot over her saddle horn and leaped straight down to the ground—a most unladylike maneuver, although she performed it with admirable grace.

"And it's one hell of a job, I'm afraid!"

She laughed and showed no embarrassment about her earthy tongue. Removing one of her doeskin riding gloves, she walked up to Longarm and stuck out her hand.

"Marshal Long, I'm pleased to meet you."

"Nonsense, Miss Colby." Longarm, removed his hat, squeezed her delicate hand, and gave a gentlemanly bow. "The pleasure is mine."

She gave a little, mock-courtly bow in return, bending her knees. "Did you have a nice trip?"

"Fair," he said, reminded of the stage's demise. He'd have to inform Colby of that, since the man had assumed the position of town marshal here in San Simon. "Just fair. And hot."

"It is a long trip down from the Panhandle, I know. I came that route, as well, and then suffered the three-day stage ride through the desert. But that was a long time ago, when I was just a girl. Haven't been away from here since. Father likes to keep me close to home, don't you know."

She laughed, and Longarm noticed her eyes flicking clandestinely across him, sizing him up ever so subtly. He followed suit, enjoying the way she filled out her soft blue shirt and tight jeans that caressed her thighs and hips in a way that made his hands want to do the same.

"Couldn't have been that long ago," Longarm said, smiling, holding his hat in his hand against his chest. "Why, you can't be over . . . oh, I'd say . . . seventeen?"

She blushed again and lowered her eyes, bashfully.

"My daughter is thirty years old, Marshal Long," said the major, looking admiringly down from his perch atop the jailhouse veranda. "Doesn't look it, though, does she?"

Longarm was honestly surprised. Only when he looked very close could he see a few stray lines around her eyes, maybe an ever-so-slight tightening around her lips. But the eyes themselves owned the bright innocence of a young girl, perhaps even a child, untempered by the crudeness of the woman's surroundings.

Could she be a little touched?

If so, she may have come by it honestly, for the major's own eyes were none too sane.

"Pshaw!" Longarm said. "Really?"

"I think it's all the fresh, dry air and this beautiful

sunshine," Clara said. "As well as all the work a girl must do to run a household on a remote frontier outpost, even one populated by only her father and herself."

She beamed lovingly up at her father. He returned the look.

"I'm sorry that I brought only enough food for you, Father. You be a good boy now and share with Marshal Long!" This with feigned admonishment as she handed the basket up to the major.

"That's not necessary," Longarm said, though he could smell the food—roasted beef and onion sandwiches—nestled under the oilcloth, and it made his belly stir. "I was just fixin' to scout out an eaterie. I could go with a plate of carne asada."

"Nonsense. There's plenty here for both of us, Marshal." The major held the basket in one hand while lifting the oilcloth with the other. "My daughter stocks my lunch baskets with enough grub to fill a track layer's larder!"

The girl swung to Longarm and extended her hand once more, smiling so brightly that Longarm thought she'd soon sprout wings and become airborne, her pert breasts dancing around inside of her soft, muslin blouse.

"It was so nice to meet you, Marshal Long. If you have no other place to stay and don't mind a touch of crudeness, I hope you'll consider our place at the outpost. It's small but comfortable, and I do try to kill the cockroaches and kangaroo rats as fast as they slither between the bricks!"

Her snicker was like the tinkle of spring raindrops on the side of a tin tub hanging on the outside of a cabin wall.

"Haven't made any arrangements just yet," Longarm said.

"But I'm sure he'll consider the offer," the major said. "We do have much business to discuss, after all, so we might as well be housed together during the course of your stay here around San Simon."

"Good!" The girl swung lithely onto her horse's back, throwing back her shoulders and sticking her breasts out; the blouse drew taut across the two firm mounds. "Can I expect you for supper, then?"

"If it's not too much trouble, I reckon I'd be downright rude to refuse such an offer, Miss Colby."

"Clara."

"Then please call me, Longarm."

"Till this evening, Longarm!"

The girl swung her horse around, touched steel to its flanks, and galloped back in the direction from which she'd come.

Puffing his pipe, the major moved off the jailhouse porch, holding the wicker basket straight down by his side. "Come along, Marshal. Let's head over to the cantina yonder, and get us a couple of drinks to go with our meal. I meant what I said. Clara's got enough food here to feed a field crew."

Longarm shucked his Winchester from his saddle boot and set it on his shoulder as he turned to follow the major toward a low-slung, cream adobe set back behind a stone wall that encompassed a dusty patio under a ramada of woven mesquite branches. The place bore no sign, but there were several gents, mostly Mexicans, though also a couple of Anglos in rough trail garb, sitting at the several crude wooden tables, drinking and eating tacos.

As they crossed the street, a man's call rose on Longarm's left. He turned to see the two soldiers he'd seen earlier slouching toward him with St. Vince's fat body slumped between them. One man was carrying the killer by his arms, the other by his legs, both shuffling sideways toward the jailhouse. Apparently, they'd pulled the fat killer's pants up but hadn't bothered buckling his belt, so the trousers had tumbled back down to his thighs, his large pale, hairy ass dragging along the street, his pale belly hanging out.

"What you want us to do with him, Major?" asked the sergeant in the palm-leaf sombrero, a loosely rolled quirley dangling from between his lips.

The major had stopped in the middle of the street. "Haul him out to the post, bury him behind the cemetery. Don't bother with a marker. Men like that don't deserve to have their graves marked!"

He scowled and then continued through the gap in the wall to the patio. When Longarm and the major had slumped into chairs at a table under the brush arbor, the eyes of the four other customers in the place regarding the newcomer suspiciously, a fat Mexican woman in a shapeless, thread-bare purple gown brought them each a wooden cup of pulque, a traditional alcoholic beverage made from the sap of the maguey plant. Before she left, the major asked her for a couple of plates. Longarm doffed his hat and ran a brusque hand through his close-cropped hair.

"Major, concerning the stage I was on," he said as Colby peeled the oilcloth from over the wicker basket.

"Yes, I was wondering about that." The major paused as the Mexican woman set two tin plates on their table. When she went away, he continued with: "I noticed that grullo you rode in on wore the brand of Sam Quine's Three Forks outfit."

"Quine gave me the horse after the stage ended up at the bottom of the Rio Grande."

Colby had just set on a tin plate half of a fat sandwich from which thick chunks of venison oozed, and he shoved the plate toward Longarm. His face clouded up, eyes pinching devilishly. "Señorita Revenge!"

Longarm shook his head. "I don't think so. Apparently, some hombre named Marquez is after Quine's daughter."

"Oh, yes . . . Marquez." Colby looked only slightly relieved. "A bandito from the other side of the Rio Grande. I've been trying to catch him on this side of the river, so I can hang him and all his cold-blooded gang of rapists, horse and cattle thieves, but my trouble with him is the same as the one I have with Señorita Revenge. I'm afraid I'm short on good trackers, and my hands are tied when it comes to crossing the border."

"As you probably know, the U.S. Marshals office received permission from the Mexican government to investigate the situation."

"Yes, I suppose I could send men out of uniforms across, but . . ."

"Not without risking them getting shot as spies." The Mexicans were adamant about not allowing American soldiers, in or out of uniform, on Mexican soil. They saw it as a form of imperialistic aggression. But President Johnson's cabinet had managed to work out agreements, on a case-by-case basis. Federal lawmen, however, could cross the border to investigate crimes committed by outlaws and Indians who nettled the citizens of both countries and who crossed the border seeking apparent sanctuary.

As they ate the thick sandwiches and the potato salad that Clara had provided, Longarm more thoroughly reported on Marquez's attack on the stage. That bit of business finished, he asked the major to delineate the crimes committed by Señorita Revenge. When the major had told him about the various stage holdups and had given a general summation of her party's attacks on his regular patrols, he said, "One ambush earlier this spring, about four months ago, was the worst of all."

Chewing the succulent beef and crusty brown bread, Longarm looked over his sandwich at Major Colby, who was forking potato salad into his mouth. The major had just cleared his throat to speak when a voice said behind them, "The worst, Major? Oh, I wouldn't say the *worst*. At least, she left one of us alive."

The major glanced back at the man in cavalry blues standing in the cantina's open door, arms crossed on his chest as he leaned against the frame. He was a handsome, dark-haired soldier with a thick, dark brown mustache and stylish muttonchop whiskers. On his shoulders were captain's bars. He wore a tan kepi slightly low on his forehead, so that the brim sat down over his brows. Beneath the brim, his brown eyes owned a wry, glassy cast.

"Ah, Captain Stockley," Colby said. "I'd forgotten it was your day off. Come, please join us. I'd like you to meet someone."

The captain pushed away from the door frame and walked toward Longarm and Colby's table, his lips pressed in a hard line beneath his mustache. He gazed at Longarm. "No need for formal introductions, Major. The gentleman's reputation proceeds him, as well as his description. A tall drink of water in tweed, with a sidearm holstered high on the left. You must be Deputy U.S. Marshal Custis P. Long—more commonly referred to in most of the newspaper articles as Longarm." He grinned, jeering. "*The long arm of the law,* who always gets his man."

Longarm stood, wiping the crumbs from his mustache with a cloth napkin, and shook the man's hand. "Nice to meet you, Captain."

"Call me Jim." The captain turned and called into the cantina, "Rosie, bring my bottle, will you? And the beer." To Longarm, he said, slurring his words slightly though he appeared to be a man who'd learned to hold his liquor from long practice, "Like the major said, it's my day off. And there isn't much to do around here on your day off but drink."

He sagged into a chair, Colby on his left, Longarm on his right. Flies hovered around his head, buzzing. He removed his hat and waved it at them viciously, scowling. "Bastards. Get the hell out of here. Find someone else's blood to suck!"

Longarm felt his lower jaw hang when he saw the scar on the captain's forehead. It was a deep, grizly wound, now mounded with a thick, brown scab and owning the shape of a large numeral 8. "Holy Christ," the federal lawman said. "How in the devil did you get that nasty tattoo, Captain?"

"What tattoo?" The captain set his hat on the table and looked at Longarm with mock befuddlement.

Then he laughed, throwing his head back and startling the thick Mexican woman, Rosie, who shook her head and glowered as she set a half-empty schooner of beer and a half-empty tequila bottle on the table near Captain Stockley. Muttering in Spanish, she walked away.

Stockly pointed at the grisly scar that oozed puss from its edges. "That there is courtesy of Señorita Revenge. Ain't she a caution?" The captain laughed again.

Major Colby regarded the man with disgust, then turned to Longarm. "The captain had a patrol out scouting the Comanche Trail southwest of here when he was hit unexpectedly. He alone survived. Señorita Revenge herself carved that number eight into his forehead and then put the captain on a horse. One of the outpost guards saw the horse trotting across the desert at dusk, heading for the barns."

Longarm glanced at Stockley, who was taking a long, deep pull from his beer schooner. "How many others killed?"

"Nine, including a good sergeant, Buff Whitaker, and two scouts. We never did find the scouts. Likely, they became wolf bait."

Longarm looked at the captain's grisly forehead. "What's the significance of that eight?"

"We been all over that," Colby said. "Haven't a clue. At first, we thought maybe it was the number of men she'd killed that day, sparing Stockley, but there were more than eight. Who knows?" The major shrugged and sat back in his chair, leaving a bite of his sandwich on his plate. "Maybe it's some sort of Kiowa symbol or talisman. Whatever it is, the captain says she has one herself. On her chest." He smiled smokily. "Above a nice pair of Injun bosoms."

Longarm looked at Stockley, who nodded. "I guess this makes us betrothed to one another, eh?"

Longarm raked a thumbnail along his unshaven jaw, pondering the information. Now he was as confused as ever. He felt genuinely sick for the captain. Not only did the wound look sore as hell, but no man wanted to walk around for the rest of his life with a scar that size and of that curious shape on his forehead.

Obviously, Stockley had not taken it well, and that was due in no small part to what it represented for him—shame. His life had likely been spared by a fierce enemy for the sole purpose of humiliating him for the rest of his days . . . or, possibly, to send a message to his ilk. But every time he looked in the mirror to shave, he'd be reminded of that massacre. The men under him who'd died.

The man was gaunt and pale, his shoulder slumped, which prompted Longarm to ask, "Any other wounds, Captain?"

"I took an arrow in the back. Damn near killed me, but not quite. Oh, not quite. I'm still here." Stockley sighed.

"Have any of the señorita's other victims been similarly marked?" Longarm inquired.

"No," said Colby. "At least none whose bodies have been recovered. Just the captain."

"What the hell did I ever do to her?" Stockley said with a sigh, leaning back in his chair. The scar couldn't have been more obvious if it had been embroidered in gold, the sunlight catching it.

"Thanks for the sandwich," Longarm told the major, sliding his plate away and washing the last bite down with the pulque, which tasted faintly of milk and grapefruit juice but with the power of a mule's kick. He'd only had half his glass, and already the day was acquiring the bleached colors of a waking dream. Any more, and he'd have to have a long nap.

Making an effort to keep his mind sharp, he said, "Let's get down to the nitty-gritty here, fellas." He glanced from the drunken Stockley to Colby, turning the wooden cup in both his big, brown hands, his Winchester leaning against the table on his right. "Give me your theories on why she's targeting this area, and seems to be targeting the men from the Sotol Creek outpost in particular."

The major and the captain both shared a look. Then Colby hiked a shoulder. "Because we're here, most likely. I think it's obvious she's trying to take land back for her people, or she's simply exacting revenge for us being here, on land she believes is her own."

Longarm looked at Stockley, sitting back in his chair with a wry, drunk look on his otherwise handsome face—a man of good breeding, most likely. A Yankee, judging by his hard consonants, who hailed from the East. Stockley lifted his hands, palms up.

"Come on," Longarm urged. "She didn't give you any other indication when she was carving that tattoo?"

"I'd passed out, thank Christ," Stockley said. "She'd punched an arrow through my back. All I remember is a burning feeling in my head. When I woke up, I was tied belly-down over my horse, and we were heading back toward Sotol Creek. I was hoping I'd bleed to death so I wouldn't have to endure this indignity."

The defeated man chuckled, took a long pull on his tequila bottle, and chuckled again. "It wasn't like we were outnumbered. I just wasn't ready. Saw no sign all that day or the day before. I'd played right into her hands, rode right into that ambush." He rolled his drink-bleary eyes toward the major. "You really oughta stand me up in front of the nearest wall and shoot me."

"Nonsense," Colby said, reaching over to place a comforting hand on the captain's shoulder. "She's a sneaky bitch. Devilish. Born to this rocky desert. She and her warriors don't fight like civilized men. What happened to you, Jim, is you were in the wrong place at the wrong time. Forget about it now. I'm short on men, Fort Stockton has no more soldiers to spare, and regimental headquarters' idea of helping out was to send a lone federal lawmen to help track that catamount down. I need every ounce of every man I've got!"

Stockley's eyes glazed with emotion. He covered it with another ironic chuckle, and then threw back another couple of tequila shots from the bottle. He sat back in his chair and stared at the table, as though his mind were slipping off, fleeing far, far away from this dusty village only a few miles north of the Rio Grande.

Longarm looked at Colby. "How many are in the señorita's gang?"

"Stockley said around nine. That number matches the unshod horse prints we've found around the other massacres and the stage coaches she's attacked."

"Marshal Vail told me she hasn't killed any civilians. She just robs them, humiliates them. She's only killed army men."

"So far," Colby said.

"The number eight doesn't match any numbers associated with the outpost?" Longarm looked around, trying to pull rabbits out of the proverbial hat. "Regiment number? Battalion? Maybe a barracks number?"

"No, no. The men stationed here are from companies A and E of the Third Cavalry."

Longarm decided the eight probably was, as Stockley had opined, a Kiowa talisman of some kind. Maybe a family or tribal emblem.

"Any idea where she holes up when she's not killing soldiers?" he asked.

"Likely part of the time in Mexico, the other part in the Chisos. Whenever I send men out these days, I lose them, so I'm not sending them out anymore. That's why headquarters sent for you."

"Well, one man likely has a better chance of tracking her unseen," Longarm said. After all, he'd done similar things before.

Colby drew a deep breath, throwing his shoulders back. He had the aura of a man trying to bear up under an enormous weight. The fact that his bedeviler was female likely quadrupled his frustration and humiliation, as it probably did for all the soldiers at the Sotol Creek outpost, where morale was likely about as low as it could get.

"Every scout I've sent out after her has come back dead, tied over his horse, just like the captain. They've been badly tortured, left to die slowly. I've stopped sending even scouts. My guess is that at the moment she's somewhere in Mexico, though I deeply believe she's half-animal. Maybe all animal. Mountain lion.

"She probably stays on the run, which makes her damn near impossible to track. She lurks around, waiting for another opportunity to butcher my men. Hell . . ." The major looked around, wrinkling the skin above the bridge of his sun-browned nose, wary. "Maybe she's nearby, watching us right now. From one of them ridges around the town . . ."

Longarm followed the man's gaze to the cactus-bristled hills rolling away beyond the town toward the rugged, sandstone ridges of the Chisos Mountains.

Colby pinned Longarm with a flat look, his dark eyes seething with desperation. "Now it's your turn to attempt to find her. And kill her."

"One man . . ." Stockley had roused himself enough for another caustic laugh. "I know your reputation, Marshal. But your boss has sent you on a suicide mission."

Longarm threw back the last of his pulque, winced as the harsh liquor seared past his vocal cords before plunging its fire down his throat and into his belly. "Yeah, well, I've had a few of those before," he said in a pinched voice. "What's she look like?"

"Beautiful," said Stockley, in a low, level voice, as if her beauty only added to the puzzling nature of the girl's depravity, as well as the number she wore on her breast and had tattooed into his forehead. "Thick black hair. Fine-featured face. Full, beautiful breasts. Skin like varnished cherry. She has a beauty mark right here."

He pressed a finger to the left side of his mouth.

Longarm stared at him, befuddled. Then he gazed off into the hazy distance beyond the town. Stockley had just described Valencia Quine.

He was about to ask him and Colby if they'd seen Quine's Mexican daughter, if they knew the story of her adoption, when a gun barked somewhere east along the

village's rutted, sun-drenched main street. Longarm jerked
to life, even against the waylaying hand of the pulque. He
automatically reached for his holstered .44, but he left the
gun in its holster as he, Stockley, and Colby looked around.
The blast had been muffled by the walls of a building on
the far side of the street.

A man screamed shrilly, and then another two gunshots
resounded around the town.

Chapter 9

Silence descended in the wake of the pistol fire. The sun continued to rain down on the street like liquid gold.

Somewhere off in the hills around the town, a dog began barking. A baby cried. It was so hot and dry that no one was in the street, but Longarm saw a few men slumped in the shade on each side of it, one fanning himself with his sombrero.

No one stirred. A couple of the loafers looked around idly, vaguely curious. A shopkeeper appeared in the doorway of his store, looked up the street to the east, shrugged, and ducked back into the place.

"At ease, Marshal," said Colby, lounging back in his chair with a self-satisfied expression. "I have several men on patrol. They'll check it . . ."

He let his voice trail off as his eyes focused on something behind Longarm, eastward along the street. Stockley blinked as though to clear dust from his eyes, and then he looked in the same direction as the major, over Longarm's right shoulder. Longarm craned his head in time to see a ragged little man in a broadcloth coat stumble out of a break between two buildings about a hundred yards away.

The little man had long, dark-brown hair and a beard, and he was sporting an eye patch. Something shiny flashed on his chest. He fell in the street with a yelp and grabbed the back of his left thigh. A man in cavalry blues stepped out of the break behind him. Another man in cavalry blues rode a bay horse out of a break a little farther east and turned the horse toward the soldier on foot and the little man in the street.

Longarm glanced at Colby, who sat back in his chair, nodding slowly with satisfaction, narrowing his eyes against the sun. When Longarm returned his gaze to the east, he saw the mounted soldier and the one on foot hazing the little, dark-haired man up the street toward the jailhouse. The little man was limping and grunting and cursing in Spanish. The soldier on foot prodded him with his pistol, giving him frequent swipes across the shoulder with the pistol's butt. The man on horse rode a little behind, holding a carbine across his saddlebow.

As they drew to within fifty feet of the cantina, Colby slid his chair back, slowly rose, and walked over to the low stone wall. The two soldiers saw him and stopped, the one on foot grabbing the collar of the ragged little man and turning him toward the major.

"Major Colby," the soldier on foot said, grinning. He was stocky and blond, with blue eyes and a bleached out goat beard. "Look who we found skulkin' around north of town."

"Juan Santana, you old horse thief," said Colby. "How dare you step foot in my town again!"

"He was visiting his whore," said the man on horseback, showing two silver front teeth as he grinned. Like the soldier on foot, he was a private. "What you want we should do with him, Major?"

"You know what to do with him."

Longarm frowned, curious, apprehensive. He hadn't liked the major's tone when he'd said that last. A half second later, when a pistol barked, cutting through the heavy, afternoon silence, he knew why.

He watched in shock as the ragged little man's head jerked forward. The man stumbled ahead, dropped to his knees, and fell flat on his face in the street, onto the stain made by his own blood and blown-out brains.

The stocky private lowered his smoking pistol, grinning. The mounted rider drew back on the reins of his bay that had been startled by the sudden blast. He, too, grinned.

"Leave him there," Colby said, digging his pipe out of his shirt pocket, "as a warning to any of his gang milling about my town."

The two men saluted.

"Stay on patrol," Colby said.

The two swung around and drifted back toward the heart of San Simon.

Longarm turned toward Stockley, who merely smiled grimly and hiked a shoulder. As the major returned to the table, puffing his pipe, Longarm said, "That was a cold-blooded killin' I just witnessed, Colby. That man had a right to a fair trial."

"Stay out of it, Marshal." Colby spoke lazily, puffing his pipe, the flame of a lucifer match dancing over the eagle's head bowl. "We do things differently out here. Have to, or the border bandits would overrun the place." He sat down and tossed the match onto the patio's cracked flagstones. "I tried doin' it right when I first took over for the town's dead lawmen. Between visits of the circuit court judge, my jail got so full I was housin' prisoners in a livery barn. Then the judge got shot out on the desert. We found his bleached carcass in a dry arroyo, identified him by his cheap suit and the law books in his leather grip."

Colby shook his head and chuckled. "I know it's startling to see. But I either do things this way or give the town back to the Mexicans. I'm trying to bring civilization to the Big Bend. Why don't you ride on over to the outpost, Marshal? My daughter will show you a mineral springs behind the house. There's several around here. The water's supposed to be right restorative as well as cleansing. I know I've found it so."

He puffed his pipe, regarding Longarm with those eyes filled with subtle but off-putting folly, like the eyes of a prisoner who'd been too long in isolation.

"How long you been out here, Major?" Longarm asked.

Colby puffed his pipe, thinking about it. "Damn, must be nigh on fifteen years now." The figure seemed to surprise even him; he gave a bemused snort, shook his head, and returned the meerschaum pipe to his mouth.

Longarm glanced once more at the raggedy little man lying facedown in the street. A spotted dog was sniffing the wound in the dead man's skull.

Longarm didn't like Colby and the man's brand of vigilante justice. He wasn't sure yet about Stockley. But he knew he needed to find out more about both these men. By so doing he might find out why Señorita Revenge had drawn such a large target on the Sotol Creek outpost.

"I believe I'll take you up on your offer, Major." Longarm grabbed his rifle and heaved himself up out of his chair.

The major gave him directions to his quarters at the outpost. Longarm pinched his hat brim to both Colby and Stockley, then crossed the street, mounted the grullo, and rode on out of San Simon.

He might be able to find out more about Colby and the post in general from the man's daughter.

A storm was building. Longarm could feel it in the air, an electricity that permeated the heat and made his hair ends sizzle.

A plum-colored anvil was taking shape over the Chisos Mountains beyond the outpost, but that was another kind of storm. That one might or might not reach Sotol Creek and San Simon. It could head north or west or even south.

The other one, however, the one he could feel building like the slow detonation of several dynamite kegs, was already here. The silence of it was ominous, for it was the silence of that split second between the fuse burning out and the dynamite igniting.

The unease squirmed around in him as the grullo followed the well-churned wheel ruts through the rocks and the bayonet-like spikes of sotol cactus, some thrusting up over six feet tall, west of the village. The heat blasted down on him, dried him out like jerky left too long in the stove. He could feel the heat through his hat. He stared at the storm cloud building over the mountains, wishing it would roll this way, cool it off some, maybe soften the air with a little moisture.

Señorita Revenge . . .

Who the hell was she? What was she so angry about? Something told Longarm that she had her neck in a bulge about more than just the intrusion on her territory. And the fact that her description had fit that of Valencia Quine was part of what caused that feeling of an unseen storm building, caused his nerves to sizzle. The other cause was Colby's seeming stranglehold on the town, if not the entire area, though he now seemed to be in competition with the savage little Kiowa gal, who was confounding him no end.

A man like Colby was especially dangerous when frustrated. Barring the number of men needed to wage an all-out war on the Kiowa, was he taking his frustration out on San Simon? The Anglo settlers and businessmen might think the major's iron fist was just what the country needed. But what about the Mexicans?

Ahead, lean-tos of dirty cream canvas fluttered in the breeze, on the other side of the nearly dry creek that snaked along at the bottom of a six-foot-deep arroyo. Longarm saw several such lean-tos situated between the creek and the outpost of what appeared to be crumbling adobe brick buildings arranged around a barren parade ground, the American flag buffeted from a cottonwood pole in the center.

The lean-tos completely surrounded the outpost, maybe sixty yards apart. Likely, guards armed with field glasses and rifles hunkered in each one—scouting for Kiowa. There was no stockade around the outpost, no guard towers, which was not unusual for outposts this far out in the back country.

From a chair inside the lean-to nearest the wooden bridge Longarm now clomped across, a man rose up and raised his Spencer carbine. A scraggly cottonwood feebly shaded him. He was smoking a quirley. His uniform was ragged, and his eyelids drooped wearily. Weary from the isolation and the dust and the heat, no doubt. As well as from the Indian scare.

"What's your business here, partner?"

Longarm told him. The man gave him brief directions to the major's quarters and sat back down in his slat-bottom chair inside the lean-to, smoking and staring tiredly into the southern distance.

Longarm booted the grullo on across the bridge. He skirted the parade ground and the crumbling adobes and cottonwood structures, including a barbershop and a sutler's store, and headed northward along a wagon trail. The smell of rotten trash and overfilled latrines was heavy on the hot, dry breeze. It was a smell that haunted every outpost Longarm had ever visited, and it made him wonder again at Clara Colby's optimism and affable innocence.

He followed the trail out behind the quartermaster's and commissary storehouses, and onto a slight rise where a two-story adobe-brick house sat behind a brush-roofed ramada. They were crude but not unpleasant looking quarters hunched in the shade of two large cottonwoods, one abutting each end. A dry fountain stood before it, in the horseshoe formed by the circular wagon path.

Down the rocky, mesquite-stippled slope behind the house lay several stables, hay barns, and cottonwood pole corrals, as well as the crude adobe quarters of the camp hostlers and horse breakers. They were far enough away, a hundred yards or so, to give the commander's house some privacy. Longarm could hear soldiers talking as they milled among the barn and corrals, some tending horses, but otherwise there was only the sound of quail piping in the rocks and mesquites flanking the house.

"Miss Colby?" he called as he checked the grullo down near the hitch rack shaded by the brush ramada's overhang.

The place's real glass windows were dark, reflecting the brassy afternoon sunlight. A clay ojo hung from the ramada's rafters, turning lazily in the breeze. Longarm called again. When only silence replied, he dismounted, and walked around to the back of the house, for he'd seen a low adobe wall that appeared to house a garden. It did, he saw, as he pushed through the wrought-iron gate off the house's rear corner. There were also the springs the major had mentioned, and a privy a little farther back and to the left. The springs looked like a five-by-ten-foot bathtub chipped out of the brittle sandstone—its cool, blue waters beckoning.

He walked through this little oasis to an open back door and peered into what appeared to be a kitchen, though it was so dark he couldn't see much, but he could smell the homey aroma of baking bread. He was about to knock on the cottonwood door casing when he heard what sounded like a grunt back in the kitchen's murky shadows. There was a scuffling sound.

Longarm automatically wrapped his right hand around his holstered Colt as he stepped through the door that was propped open with a rock and said, "Miss Colby?"

His voice echoed off the brick walls.

A shadow lurched out of a doorway, a curtain billowing and then falling away from a skinny soldier. A girl snickered. The curtain tore the soldier's forage hat from his head, and, casting a frightened look toward Longarm, he bent to retrieve it.

"You've . . . got company, Miss Clara," the soldier said, his voice owning a nervous trill. As Longarm's eyes grew accustomed to the thick shadows, he saw that the pink-cheeked private couldn't have been much past sixteen.

"Oh!" The girl stepped out of the curtained doorway of what Longarm assumed was a pantry and looked toward him, the light from behind him sparkling in her eyes. "Marshal Long—you're earlier than I expected!"

Chapter 10

"See ya, Miss Clara—I best get back on guard duty!" the boy said, walking backward and looking as though wolves were on his heels, before wheeling and heading for the front of the house.

"Larry, don't forget your coffee!" Clara called, reaching into the pantry for a small burlap pouch, which she held out for the boy, who snatched it out of her hands and then fairly ran out of the kitchen.

Clara turned to Longarm, who stood in the open doorway. He could feel the humorous look quirking one side of his mouth. "Sorry if I was . . . uh . . . interrupting anything, Miss Colby."

"Oh, no—of course not," she said, widening her eyes in shock. "Larry . . . I mean, Corporal Bergman . . . just came to borrow some coffee for his barracks. They're fresh out." She chuckled nervously, patting at her hair, which she'd pinned into a bun atop her head. Her blue muslin blouse was unbuttoned about halfway, showing some creamy cleavage above the embroidered top of her camisole. Her cheeks were flushed.

"Your father enticed me here for a dip in the springs," Longarm said, revising his estimation of the woman's innocence.

If she really was thirty—which he still had a hard time believing—she was wading in shallow water with young Private Bergman. One might even call such a dalliance scandalous. Longarm, of course, was no moral judge, as many of his own dalliances would be called downright appalling by those who saw themselves fit to judge, but he couldn't help wondering how much Clara's father knew about the goings on here at the house when he was in town shooting banditos.

"The springs," she said, smiling, eyes twinkling as though she adored the idea. "Of course! You saw the water. Father thinks an underground river surfaces here in a volcanic bubble of sorts and oozes off downstream through cracks in the bedrock, so the water is always new, always fresh! You can change into a bathing suit upstairs in the spare room. I'll show you!"

She started to turn away, but he stopped her with:

"I'd better tend my horse first. Then I'll haul my gear upstairs."

"Last door on the right side of the hall. My room is right across from yours. Father sleeps downstairs, when he sleeps here at all. Often, he prefers to keep an eye on things in town, so he usually beds down in one of the hotels. He prefers the one run by Señora Leonora, because the girls who work for her wash the bedding twice a week. You can put your horse in the stable here, on the west side of the house and behind the lovely pear tree I planted when I first came to this wonderful country."

She smiled so brightly, so cheerily that Longarm couldn't help thinking of a parson's wife a little tipsy on the teachings or, possibly, the communion wine. Was this all for show? Was she really as sweet and guileless as she seemed?

If so, what had she been doing with Private Bergman in the pantry earlier? She herself seemed to have forgotten it.

Longarm also couldn't help wondering what else Senora Leonora did for Major Colby, but that, like his daughter and Private Bergman, was none of his business. It was all grist for the mill, however. He pinched his hat brim to the girl—or woman, rather, as she was thirty, after all—then walked out the door and retraced the steps to his horse.

When he'd tended to the grullo, he returned to the house with his saddlebags and rifle and found the room in the second story neat and clean and with a window looking out on the springs and the little irrigated garden flanking it. He stowed his gear in the room, and having no bathing suit, he walked back out into the hall.

The door across from his opened, and Clara stepped out, holding a towel in one hand, a cigar in the other.

"Father often likes to have a cigar while he bathes," she said, as cheery as before.

"Well, I'll be hanged," Longarm said. "I was just missin' my own cheroots that the Rio Grande claimed."

"I'm so sorry!"

"All's well." He held up the cigar she'd given him. "Say, I don't have any bathing suit, so I'll be bathing in the raw. Just thought I'd warn you so you can take proper precautions."

She studied him curiously, wide-eyed, and then what he'd meant seemed to dawn on her. "Oh!" She laughed huskily. "Don't worry. I've taken my bread out of the oven—we'll have some later, when you're finished in the springs. Till then, I'll stay in my room. I'm sewing a quilt. Perhaps I'll show you later. It's wonderful to have a guest, as Father and I haven't entertained in a month of Sundays!"

With that, she stepped back into her room and closed the door.

Longarm poked the fat stogie in his mouth and walked on down the stairs and into the kitchen. Three fat, round loaves of bread steamed on a cooling rack beside the black range. The smell was almost as exhilarating as the heat was stifling. He couldn't wait to get in the water.

Outside, he looked around to make sure no one was near, then removed his pistol and shell belt and kicked out of his boots. He dropped his double-barreled derringer and the watch that was chained to it into one of his boots and began to shrug out of his frock coat.

He stopped, shrugged, and then, wearing all his clothes minus his hat and boots, he stepped down from the shelving side of the pool and into the water. He didn't doubt the girl would gladly wash his duds for him—they still sported mud from the Rio Grande—but there was a simpler method that he'd performed many, many times in the past and which worked as well as any Chinaman with a washboard.

He sank down into the water, sucking a deep breath and grinning. God, that felt good. Not cold or warm but cool enough to refresh him. He sank low in the pool, pivoting at the waist to knock as much of the mud free as he could, and then he climbed up out of the tub and shucked his clothes. Wringing out each garment one by one, he hung them all over the adobe brick wall. They'd likely dry in an hour or so, as long as it didn't rain.

When he was down to his balbriggans, he paused and looked at the house. The dark windows reflected shimmering spheres of sunlight. There was no sign of the girl. Surely, she'd stay in her room while he bathed. It wasn't proper, her being alone with a man on the place, especially one taking a dip in the springs, but apparently her father wasn't worried about her. Judging by what was happening when Longarm had first arrived, she wasn't, either.

Longarm didn't want any trouble, however. He had a job to do, and that didn't include piss-burning the camp commander by acting in any way unprofessional around the man's daughter. However, he had to admit to feeling a dull ache in his loins when he saw her blouse halfway open and that womanly flush in her cheeks.

He peeled out of the balbriggans, wrung them out, glanced at the house once more, then draped them over the wall. Quickly, he dropped back down in the pool, groaning as the cool water washed over him, peeling away about seven layers of sweat and dirt.

He sat on a shelf protruding about a foot into the pool, four feet down, then leaned forward to dunk his head and scrub his hands through his hair and scrape the grime from his ears with his fingers. When he lifted his head, blowing water and pressing it from his close-cropped hair, she was standing in the house's back door. She wore what appeared a black silk kimono. She was smiling, showing all her fine, white teeth between her pink lips.

She reached up, plucked the pins from her hair, and shook her head. The golden locks tumbled about her shoulders. The kimono was open, revealing a long pale line from her chin to her belly button. The kimono stopped at her thighs. Beneath it, she wore a pair of lacey, pink panties.

She walked toward the springs. Her breasts jostled behind the kimono, the nipples raking it from behind.

"Oh, no," Longarm said, heart thudding, loins burning. "Forget it." Indeed, she was as crazy as a tree full of owls. Beautiful, but crazy. The innocence he'd seen earlier had been replaced by a brash lustfulness.

She kept coming, taking long strides, hips swinging, both front flaps of the kimono sliding back to reveal all of her breasts except the nipples. Her smile remained.

Longarm had to take quick action. He wasn't sure what. Grab his clothes and run? Head back to San Simon and hole up in a hotel? Christ, why hadn't he done that in the first place?

He started to scramble up out of the pool. Stopping, he looked down. His cock was at half-mast, aimed right at her pink-clad pussy as she stopped at the edge of the springs. The panties were incredibly sheer. He vaguely opined that they would have fit inside one cheek and made a bulge little larger than a tobacco quid. Her thighs were long and full but not fat, her bare feet short and girlish.

"Please, don't reject me," she said as he recoiled from her and sank back down on the shelf in the springs. She shrugged out of the kimono, baring her breasts.

Quickly yet gracefully, she slid her panties down to her ankles, kicked them away and stepped into the water. He watched it slide up over her hips and flat belly. Her pink nipples pebbled as the water rose up over the bottoms of her breasts.

She flung herself against him, wrapping her arms around his neck, mashing her breasts against his chest. They were soft and cool. The nipples gently raked him. He tried to push her away from him, but she was stronger than she looked, and he didn't want to hurt her.

"Take me, Marshal. Take me here, in the springs, and then take me with you when you leave here. Oh, please!" she sobbed, tears filling her eyes.

Longarm glanced around cautiously, but the wall was at least six feet high. No one could see in.

"Don't worry—we're alone. Father sometimes has Sergeant MacKenzie's wife come over to sit with me—you know, as a chaperone, of sorts. But she has her own chores at home, and I can take care of myself just fine!"

Longarm had seen just how well she'd done that.

Again, he tried to pry her hands off the back of his neck, but she winced as though he were hurting her, and clung to him all the tighter.

"I am not a child, Marshal!"

"Maybe not in years, but you're acting like a child, Miss Clara."

"I have wants. Needs. *Desires!*"

"Miss Clara . . ."

"You're a handsome man, Marshal Long. I saw it right off. I also saw the way you looked at me when you first saw me. You imagined yourself fucking me. Don't deny it!"

Christ, Longarm thought. He'd imagined fucking nearly every woman he'd ever laid eyes on.

"Imagining it ain't the same as actually doing it. Now, Miss Clara, I understand how you're a full-grown woman and all, but I don't think you're entirely right in the head. I don't think you really know what you're doing!"

"I know exactly what I'm doing, Longarm." Her voice grew suddenly hard with anger. "And don't try to sound like the doctors!"

"*Doctors?*"

She removed one of her hands from his neck, wrapped it around his cock, and smiled again. "Do you like that?"

"No," he lied.

"God, you're *huge!*" She pumped him almost painfully, gritting her teeth. "Please, you can have me as many times as you want, as long as you promise to take me away from this awful place when you go."

Longarm dug his fingers into her arms and pushed her an arm's length away from him, until her hand slipped off of his cock. It was a move that was entirely foreign to him, but one he had to make. There were bigger things at work here than his animal need to fuck this comely young woman throwing herself at him, and he silently congratulated himself for his surprising strength of will.

He leveled a hard look at her, and it seemed to take some of the starch out of her. "What're you so damn afraid of?" Something told him it was more than the isolation and the Indian threat.

She paused, her eyes darting from left to right as she studied him carefully, as though wondering if he could understand what she had to say.

"I've been having the dreams again." She'd said it so softly that he could barely hear her above the sound of the wind in the cottonwood branches that shaded the springs. It was a haunted voice, pitched with madness.

"What dreams?"

"Dreams of that Indian girl—that savage, Señorita Revenge, they call her. She's a demon, and she and her savage warriors ride through the fort howling like wolves and killing us all with their bows and arrows, cutting our throats!"

"It's only understandable you're afraid. Have you told your father?"

"No!" She grabbed his arms, clung to him as though he were a raft in choppy seas. "If I can't stand it out here, he'll send me back to the doctors in Cincinnati! They'll put me in that place again. Oh, god—the locked rooms! The screaming!" She clapped her hands to her ears as though she could hear the screams now in her head.

Longarm felt his jaws loosen as he stared at her, not knowing what to think or what to say.

Suddenly, both hands were on his cock, gently yet fervently stroking him. Now she smiled, the bold coquette again. "I can make you feel good. I'm very good at it."

"I don't doubt that a bit," he said in a pinched voice, placing his hands on her shoulders and trying to push her away. But her eyes weakened him. Her fingers were like silk. "But I can't take you away from here, Miss Colby. You're gonna have to talk to your father about that. I bet . . . if . . . he . . . knew . . . how you really felt . . ."

Suddenly, she thrust toward him, wrapped her arms and legs around him, and he felt an undeniable wash of passion flood over him as she reached down and drew his cock into the soft, petal-like folds of flesh between her thighs. She hammered against him, and there was no denying her passion.

She grunted, mewled, groaned, desperately grinding her heels into his back. His passion rose, and he spent himself inside her. She gave a yelp as she herself attained satisfaction, and closed her mouth painfully over his shoulder, biting him hard, the pain somehow heightening the force of his climax.

He squeezed his eyes closed.

She pulled her mouth back away from his shoulder, and screamed.

Longarm opened his eyes. She was staring in wide-eyed terror at something above and behind him. In the water he saw the reflection of the war-painted Indian crouched atop the wall, drawing an arrow back against his bow, pulling the sinew taut, and aiming through slitted eyes.

Chapter 11

Longarm threw himself against the girl and forced her down, down into the springs. In the corner of his right eye, he saw the arrow smack the surface and angle down past his right shoulder before glancing off the side of the springs, small air bubbles trailing off behind its end fletched with hawk feathers.

He lifted his head above the surface and reached for his Colt holstered at the lip of the springs. With one hand, he unsnapped the keeper thong, and with his other hand he grabbed the pistol from the holster. He wheeled to see the Indian bunching his lips, brown eyes boring holes through Longarm as he nocked another arrow to his bow.

Longarm's Colt danced in his hands, the bellowing crashes echoing around the adobe walls and the back wall of the house. The Kiowa screamed and flew back off the top of the wall to hit the ground on the other side with a thud. At the same time, the girl thrust her head up out of the water and screamed, shaking her head and pressing water from her eyes with her hands.

"Stay there!"

Longarm hoisted himself out of the springs as he heard
the rattling of a distant Gatling gun. He retrieved his rifle
from where he'd leaned it against a pear tree, pumped a
fresh round into the chamber, ran naked and dripping to
the rear wall, where the Indian had crouched, and leaped
on top of it, crouching himself now and aiming the rifle
straight out from his right shoulder.

He was expecting to see an entire horde of the painted
savages sprinting toward him, but there was only the lone
brave lying on his back in the dust and rocks on the far side
of the wall, the bow and arrow lying nearby. He lay at an
awkward angle, propped against the quiver hanging down
his back, blood oozing from the hole in his naked, bronze
chest and dribbling down across his belly.

The Gatling gun sporadically wailed to the west, and
Longarm turned to see smoke rising from one of the canvas
lean-tos. Soldiers were running around, yelling, dust rising
in the westering sun that was tempered by the approaching
mass of gray-purple clouds. Out across the rocky western
flat, more dust rose. Through the dust, Longarm could see
a dozen or so dark-skinned riders jostling atop war-painted
mustangs. They angled southwest, and between bursts of
the Gatling gun, their yips and howls rose.

Longarm turned to where Clara Colby stood in the
springs, arms crossed on her breasts, clutching her shoulders and shivering. Her hair was pasted against her cheeks,
neck, and shoulders, and her terror-racked eyes held steady
on Longarm.

"We're going to die, aren't we? The dreams are coming
true!"

"Not yet."

Longarm leaped down off the wall and ran past the
springs to gather his still-wet clothes. "Get inside, Clara.
Lock yourself in your room."

"Don't leave me!"

"They're gone, Clara. For now, they're gone. I'm gonna see if I can track 'em, find out where they're goin'."

Longarm crouched over the springs, grabbed her by her shoulders, and pulled her up out of the water. The water danced across the upturned tips of her breasts with their jutting, pink nipples. "Go inside, get dried off, and lock yourself in your room. You'll be all right!"

Sobbing, she nodded, and ran naked into the house's open back door. Longarm felt like a damn fool—fucking in a springs during an Indian attack. If it really was an attack. Now he was starting to think it was more of an assassination attempt by the brave he'd killed, while the rest of the señorita's gang diverted the soldiers' attention to the west.

But why would Señorita Revenge want to kill Clara?

Longarm climbed with effort into his wet clothes, set his hat on his head, stomped into his boots, and grabbed his rifle once more. He headed for the stable, where he quickly saddled one of the other three horses snorting and stomping around owlishly in the musty shadows—a coal-black gelding he figured was fresher than the grullo that Quine had given him. Mounting up, he booted the horse out through the stable's open doors, across the hard-packed, hay-littered yard and down the hill to the west, where the rattling of the Gatling gun had died.

He passed a blacksmith shop and a barn that had an abandoned look, like many of the buildings on the forlorn outpost whose garrison had been decimated by Señorita Revenge, and down toward the gully through which Sotol Creek snaked in nearly a complete circle around the outpost. Soldiers were scurrying from their barracks near the parade ground, all wielding old carbines, toward the nest of rocks and cactus in which hunched the lean-to housing the Gatling gun.

The gunner himself, a short, red-haired youngster in a battered forage cap, now stood ahead of the lean-to, holding a Springfield rifle and staring off to the west, where the Indians had disappeared. Several other soldiers, all privates and corporals, and all looking harried, stood around him. One was yelling toward the men rushing down from the parade ground to saddle horses. Vaguely, Longarm wondered where the officer of the day was—the officer currently in charge of the fort. On most forts the officers rotated supreme authority among themselves, beneath that of the fort commander, of course.

The lawman couldn't see anyone who appeared to be in charge, though a burly, shaggy-haired, and bearded corporal who appeared to be on the far side of thirty, was doing most of the yelling as he strode in a bandy-legged gait down from the direction of the sutler's store, where he'd likely been holed up with a bottle.

Longarm slowed his horse up beside the corporal, who kept walking, holding an old, Civil War–model Lefaucheux revolver in his big left fist—a French-made pin-fire revolver that had been favored by Yankee generals and taken as a trophy by the Johnny Rebs. "Corporal, who's in charge?"

The man snapped an angry look at the lawman on the sleek black gelding. "Captain Stanley was supposed to be in charge, but I think I seen him sneak into town . . . ," the old, wryly wise man with a laurel-soft Georgia accent grinned with one half of his mouth, ". . . to make sure his girl was keepin' her panties up, if you know what I mean . . ." He frowned as he let his voice trail off. "Say, who the hell are you, anyway, and what are you doin' on the major's hoss?"

"Corporal, keep all the soldiers here at the fort!" Longarm rammed his heels against the black's ribs. "I'm gonna track those Kiowa, but they might be settin' a trap! Inform Major Colby and stay alert!''

"Hey," the corporal bellowed as Longarm galloped past the red-haired private who'd been firing on the Kiowa, "who in thunder are you, anyways?"

His voice was drowned by the thudding of the black's hooves.

Longarm hoped the mount was a good jumper, because there was no near bridge across the creek. As they approached the cutbank's edge, the soldiers eyeing him skeptically, the black gave a whinny and leaped off its back hooves, expertly spanning the ten-foot-wide gully, and landing without a hitch on the other side. The horse had hardly broken stride before it was galloping off again to the west, where Longarm could see the feathery tan cloud of sifting dust kicked up by the fleeing Kiowa.

He pushed the horse hard through the sandy desert. When he picked up the Indians' trail, he pushed harder, and followed the tracks of a dozen unshod horses through a low jog of hills rolling up toward the foothills of the Chisos Mountains. The cloud over the mountains grew larger and darker, and it became lightning-stitched. He could see the massive gray shadow angling down over the side of the range and extending out into the plain, though he was still at least a mile away from it.

The gray veil drifting down from the cloud mass meant it was raining up there. Likely, the arroyos around him would be filled soon. He pushed on, wanting to get some idea of where the Indians were headed. There wasn't much water out here, so they were limited in their choice of bivouacs. They probably had several springs dotting their travel routes, which likely led by way of the springs to the Rio Grande and across into Mexico.

The Chisos Range shouldered on his right. It looked

like a giant corduroy hat. A purple one, with that shadow over it. Around him, the country was all bluffs and sweeping mesas and sun-beached rocks and cactus. The sun hammered down on him, drying his clothes, burning through him. He didn't have a canteen or any other trail supplies, so he couldn't make this a long pull, but if he could locate one of the Kiowa raiding party's travel routes, he'd be a couple of chips ahead of the game.

Longarm drew back on the black's reins. The horse ground its hooves into the chalky sand and soil, skidding to a stop and kicking up a thick dust cloud. Longarm stared ahead through a deep crease between steep buttes. Far ahead in the crease, where it opened out into sunlight, dust wafted.

Longarm stared at that lacy mare's tail of sifting dust. The hair under his collar pricked. He'd just started to neck rein the black sharply to his right when an Indian stepped out from a boulder on the crease's left side, about fifty yards ahead of him.

Ambush!

The brave jerked a Winchester carbine to his shoulder. Longarm crouched low in the saddle as the rifle screeched shrilly around the crease. The Indian's slug blasted a rock along the shoulder of the bluff now on Longarm's left as he ground his heels into the black's flanks.

The horse galloped through a crease leading north from the Indians' trail. After fifty yards, Longarm jerked back on the reins again, leaped out of the saddle, and quickly tied the horse to a mesquite root in the shade of a stone overhang. He ran up the side of a bluff, then edged around its shoulder, stopping only a few feet shy of the crest.

He licked his dry lips and edged a look up and over the ridge crest. In the crease below, a young, muscular Kiowa buck, in deerskins and with a red flannel bandanna holding his long, black hair back from his face, was hunkered in a thin patch of dry brush, glaring up toward Longarm.

The Kiowa's eyes flashed as he raised his Spencer repeater. Longarm pulled back behind the bluff's lip as the Spencer howled, its slug blowing up dust a foot from where his face had just been. Hearing the Kiowa ejecting the spent cartridge casing, Longarm lurched forward once more, aimed quickly over the sloping crest of the butte, and fired.

He cursed as his bullet smashed the rock behind which the Kiowa dove as he headed into another notch between the stony buttes that were shaped like dinosaur teeth, jutting in all directions. Longarm threw caution to the wind as he bounded over the top of the ridge and went running down the other side, loosing rocks and gravel in his wake.

He was here now, and he wasn't getting out of here until all the Indians who'd held back to ambush him were dead. Of course, the entire gang might be holed up in these rocks, and if that were true, and if they were all as strapping as the buck nearest him now, he was as good as dead. He hoped that only a few had stayed back.

He dropped down into the narrow valley between the buttes and ran down an intersecting one, after the last ambusher. Ahead, the brave was running up the slope on Longarm's left, angling toward a boulder. Longarm stopped and triggered two quick shots, his slugs blowing up dirt and gravel off the Indian's moccasin-clad heels. A third shot screeched off the face of the boulder he'd just ducked behind.

Hooves and a man's labored breath sounded behind Longarm.

He wheeled to see an Indian on a wild-eyed mustang galloping toward him, another brave running alongside the horse. The man on horseback was nocking an arrow to his bow, riding with his rope reins in his teeth. The other brave carried a rifle, two big knives bristling in sheaths strapped to his thighs. Their faces were both war masks of painted lines and swirls. They were both as strapping as the first.

The brave hunkered behind the boulder fired his Spencer as Longarm dropped to a knee beside a broad barrel cactus. The slug ripped chunks from the side of the cactus as Longarm snugged his rifle to his shoulder and triggered the Winchester until its hammer pinged on an empty chamber. Through his own wafting powder smoke he saw the horseback brave fly off the back of his horse a half second after he'd loosed the arrow, which slammed into the side of the cactus, only inches from Longarm's right shoulder.

The brave hit the ground with a grunt. Longarm couldn't tell if he'd hit him, but the brave crabbed off into some rocks and brush like an ochre-painted coyote. The other brave ducked behind a boulder and snaked his rifle over the top of it. Longarm threw himself straight back between two boulders on his left and winced as the Indian's slugs hammered the front of each boulder.

Longarm looked around as he quickly thumbed fresh shells through the Winchester's loading gate. A pale game trail snaked up the ridge above him. There were plenty of rocks there for cover.

Hearing the raspy breaths and quick footfalls of the brave with the bow and the one on foot with the carbine trying to work around him, he leaped to his feet, fired the Winchester twice at where instinct told him the two nearest braves were, then took off running up the steep hill. He wove around the rocks, grinding his teeth as the two braves with rifles opened up on him. An arrow slammed into the side of an ironwood shrub, which meant the brave who'd leaped off the mustang was still relatively healthy.

The mustang itself continued thundering straight on down the main crease between the hills, giving an angry whinny and trailing its rope reins, dust roiling behind it. Breath wheezing in and out of his laboring lungs, Longarm hunkered low as he scrambled through a relatively open area, heading for a wagon-sized boulder perched on the side of the hill. He was ten feet from cover when the angry bee of a half ounce of lead stung his left calf.

It felt as though that leg had been clubbed with an axe handle. It was a pounding burn. He dropped to his knees and elbows, started rolling down the slope to his left, and released his rifle to reach for a rock to stop himself.

The tips of his fingers scraped painfully across the side of the rock, and he continued rolling down the hill facing the crease where he knew at least two of his Kiowa assailants were.

"Shit!" he heard himself rake out as the two braves with rifles opened up on him in earnest.

Chapter 12

One slug blew up dust about four inches in front of Long-arm's forehead, spraying his face with sand and gravel. Another hammered the ground a half second before his belly landed on the same small crater. He could feel the heat of the bullet against his belly button, but it was nothing compared to the heavy pain in his left calf.

Gritting his teeth as an arrow cracked off the side of a boulder, he threw himself behind another boulder and slid his Colt from its holster. He snaked the pistol around the boulder just as the brave he'd chased into the crease bounded out from behind his cover and started scrambling down the hill on the other side of the crease from Longarm.

The brave must have thought Longarm's goose was cooked, because he looked surprised when he saw the pistol aimed at him. His own momentum was carrying him too quickly down the hill for him to stop. When the slug hammered through the dead center of his chest, he threw his Spencer forward, as though it had grown suddenly too hot to hold, and fell back against the side of the hill on his butt with a grunt.

He grabbed the bloody hole in his chest with both hands before slumping sideways and rolling.

A fierce yowling rose above Longarm on his left. He wheeled to see the brave with the bow and arrow running toward him, a big bowie-like knife in his fist. Longarm triggered his Colt, but in his haste he sailed the slug into the slope just right of the running Kiowa. Before he could squeeze the trigger again, the Kiowa rammed his right fist against the underside of Longarm's wrist.

The pistol sailed up over his head, flashing in the sunlight.

The Indian grinned and drew his hand to one side before slashing it forward and sideways, intending to cut the white man's throat. Before he could begin thrusting the knife forward, however, Longarm slammed his right boot hard against the brave's right kneecap.

There was an audible *crack!*

The Indian groaned and glanced down at his badly hyper-extended leg.

Longarm bounded up and forward, springing off his heels, and bulled the Indian over backward. The brave gave a keening screech that rattled Longarm's brains, and slammed his left elbow against the lawman's right cheek, causing white doves to flutter in front of Longarm's eyes. The brave forced Longarm onto his back, punched him twice—hard, quick jabs with his clenched fist—and then Longarm returned the blows. Two rights and a hard left jab, and then the Indian, who was built like a bulldog, with powerful legs and shoulders, bucked up savagely.

With a painful squeal as he used both legs, including the broken one, he sent the lawman sailing over his head, turning a complete somersault in the air before smashing to the ground on his back.

Longarm groaned from the concussive blow and from

the cactus and rocks spiking into his back. He heard the Indian clamoring to his feet and knew he didn't have time to brood. Scrambling up, he whipped around in time to see the stocky brave, with two ochre circles around his eyes, bulling toward him, limping on his bad leg, head down, sort of mewling, spittle flecking from his lips.

Longarm stepped sideways, grabbed the brave by his hair, and drove his head against the flat face of a boulder behind him.

There was a hard crunching *smack!* as the brave's head drove deep down into his shoulders. Still holding his hair and one arm, Longarm felt the thick, brown body go slack. He released it, and the brave dropped to his knees before rolling onto a shoulder and lying against the base of the boulder with a cracked skull, through which blood and brains oozed, and a hump in his broken neck, like that of a snake that had eaten a sizeable gopher.

Behind Longarm there rose the *click-clack* of a Spencer hammer being thumbed back to full cock. He wheeled.

Another brave, stood aiming the carbine at him, his eyes like two oily obsidian chips over the receiver, drawing a bead on Longarm. The brave's mouth quirked with satisfaction as his grimy index finger drew back on the trigger.

Ping!

The gun was empty.

The oil chips of obsidian widened in fury, and then the brave came running toward Longarm, swinging the rifle like a club. Longarm ducked. The carbine made a *whoosh* as it whipped through the air where Longarm's head had been a half second before.

Longarm rammed his right and then his left fist into the brave's belly. The brave staggered backward, dropping the Spencer. He reached for a long, curved knife sheathed on his left hip, but before he could raise the blade, Longarm was on him, wrapping both his hands around the brave's wrist, over the knife hilt.

He shoved the muscular Kiowa, who had a deeply sunken scar under his right eye, against a barrel cactus. As the brave screamed, Longarm turned the knife blade toward the brave's own washboard belly, and gave a grunt as he lunged forward. The knife's savagely tipped blade slipped through the skin beneath the Kiowa's knobby breastbone. Thick red blood washed over the blade.

Longarm gave another grunt, gritting his teeth, and thrust the blade up beneath the breastbone until he felt the slight resistance of the heart. Then he thrust again and stepped back as the brave stood there, head thrown back and wailing, blood washing over the knife, quivering as the cactus spikes held him fast while he died.

A wave of nausea caused by the blows he'd taken to the head washed over Longarm. He tried to keep his feet under him, knowing more Kiowa could be near, but suddenly the ground pitched darkly, and he sank to his butt on the gravel. He sat back against a boulder, facing the crease between the chalky buttes.

The air had cooled. The darkness wasn't just in his head. Looking up, he saw that the storm cloud had stretched out from the Chisos Range and was thrusting its shadow over him. Lightning sparked. Thunder rumbled angrily, causing the ground beneath the lawman's butt to vibrate. A cool breeze blew, drying the sweat from his face, ruffling his short hair.

He looked around carefully. No more Indians were closing on him. His pistol lay in the dust about ten feet away. He had to retrieve it, his hat, and his rifle, and get back to his horse.

As he started to rise, he stopped and pressed his back

against the side of the boulder once more. A figure stood on a turret-like chunk of butte on the other side of the crease from him, a good twenty feet up the opposite slope. His jaw slackened. His pulse quickened.

He narrowed his eyes. A young Indian woman stood atop that finger of clay and crenellated sandstone, her long, coarse, blue-black hair blowing in the cooling wind. Apprehension raked him. Strands of hair drifted over the beauty mark just left of her mouth. Her voluptuousness made his loins ache.

Valencia?

She wore a very short deerskin skirt and a skimpy, ragged-edged deerskin vest. Her legs were slender but muscled, the thighs round and hard. Moccasins rose to nearly her knees. Her arms were bare, fists on her hips. Her full bosom pushed out the vest that was held closed across them by whang strings, revealing all the long, dark cleavage between the firm, proud breasts.

A medicine pouch hung from her neck by a horsehair thong. Inside the thong, and just above where her golden cleavage started, he saw something. She was too far away for him to make it out clearly, but it looked like a pale tattoo in contrast to the penny color of the skin around it.

The image appeared similar to the one that Señorita Revenge had carved into Captain Stockley's forehead.

Longarm wanted to go for his pistol, but the girl's eyes as well as her bewitching beauty held him fast. The beauty mark just left of her lovely mouth drew wide. Her hair slid back and forth across her cheeks and her long, almond-shaped eyes that were slitted with savage cunning. Her lips were slightly pooched, her fine, long jaws set hard. The barrel of a rifle poked up from behind her right shoulder, from where it hung down her back by a leather lanyard.

Her hard, savage eyes were the only things about her

that made Longarm doubt that he was looking at Valencia Quine. They slid to either side of Longarm, taking in the three Kiowa he'd killed. When she slid her gaze back to him, she tipped her face slightly to one side, looking at him sidelong, puzzled.

"Who are you?" she said in Spanish-accented English above the sifting of the wind.

Longarm fought against the girl's mesmerizing affect on him, reminding himself who she was, all the deaths she was responsible for. He considered the many more soldiers who would die if she wasn't run to ground.

The lawman hardened his jaws. "The man who's gonna punch your ticket, señorita!" With that, he heaved himself to his feet and dove forward, his right hand coming down on his Colt .44 at the same time his belly and chest landed on the stony ground. He lifted the revolver. Raising his chin and arching his back to shoot up at a steep angle, he aimed at the clay turret, then promptly eased the tension on his trigger finger.

The girl was gone.

Storm shadows raked the pinnacle of clay and rock she'd been standing on, ripping tendrils of dust from its sides and hurling them into the cool, swirling air. The shadow grew darker, and lightning flashed wickedly. It hammered the slope behind him. It sounded like the blast of a very large pistol, causing the ground to shudder beneath him.

Longarm rose to his knees, looking around carefully, the cool wind blowing his hair, pelting him with icy raindrops. The Kiowa princess's image was slow to fade from his retinas. He'd seldom laid eyes on a girl so erotically comely. The most recent one had been back in the doomed stagecoach.

Were they one and the same?

He looked up. The sky was purple, intermittently stitched with witches' fingers of lightning followed shortly by the drumrolls of thunder. He had to get to his horse.

Quickly, he took a handkerchief from his pocket and wrapped it around his calf. Cursing, he rose and scrambled gingerly, painfully up the hill, finding his hat blown up against a sotol cactus, his rifle lying in the rocks. He loaded the Winchester as well as his Colt and then used the rifle as a crutch as he retraced his steps back in the direction of Colby's black gelding.

Unable to put much pressure on his left foot without it feeling as though a Kiowa arrow of flame was shooting up from his foot to his hip, he took over half an hour getting back to the horse that waited in the shelter, tied to the spindly mesquite root. By the time he did, rainwater was falling over the rock overhang and splashing onto the sodden ground behind the horse.

Longarm himself was once again soaked, cold, hurting, and generally miserable. As he shoved his Winchester into the saddle boot, he gave a rueful chuff. Imagine visiting the Big Bend of Texas and spending half your time soaked to the gills? Climbing onto the fidgety mount's back, he looked up through the water streaming off his hat brim.

The sky was a dense lid of gunmetal gray mottled with deep purple swirls. No letup anywhere near. The rain hammered nearly straight down at the time, threaded with small bits of hail.

"Fuck," Longarm said.

He thought it through and decided he'd head on back through the storm, lest he got stuck out here on the wrong side of a flood arroyo. He couldn't afford the lost time. He needed to get back to the Sotol Creek outpost, get his wound tended, get himself dried out, fed, whiskied, and rested, and light out first thing in the morning for Señorita Revenge.

Fortunately, the rain lightened when he'd ridden only half a mile. It lightened still more, the big purple bruise of a cloud mass rolling on to the east, taking the lightning and gradually diminishing thunder along with it. When he reached the outpost, the soldiers were on high alert, as expected, several parties in yellow rain slickers patrolling the creek bank.

Several looked so owly that Longarm thought he'd surely be shot just for being out here. He was happy when he managed to put the black across a wooden bridge and into the outpost proper, heading toward the parade ground that was pocked with fresh mud puddles. The air was freshly, heavily perfumed with piñon pine, sage, and cactus blossoms. Wood smoke touched Longarm's nostrils, and he shuddered eagerly at the thought of a warm fire.

He figured that Colby would have been told of the attack and would be manning his headquarters, which he was— smoking on the small, square, brick hovel's narrow gallery and looking much as he'd appeared when Longarm first met the man, as the sodden, wounded lawman approached on the major's black. A corporal stood near the major's office door, on guard duty with a rifle, ready for another attack by Senorita Revenge, it seemed.

"My god, man—you're alive!" the major intoned behind a billowing cloud of aromatic pipe tobacco, the scar across his left eye resembling a fat, pale worm.

Longarm half fell out of the saddle, his boots making a wet sucking sound as they dropped into the parade ground mud. "Got a shot of whiskey, Major?"

"Longarm!" This in a woman's voice. He looked up to see Clara Colby running out of the major's headquarters and down the steps. "I thought for sure that mean, old Señorita Revenge had gotten you!"

She threw herself so hard against Longarm's chest that

he stumbled back against his horse with a groan. As she buried her face in his wet wool vest and shirt, he looked up to see the major eyeing him suspiciously as the old soldier blew out a long smoke plume.

The corporal on guard duty behind him glanced from Longarm and the girl to the old man, and Longarm would have sworn the young soldier quirked a fleeting grin.

Chapter 13

Colby admonished her. "Clara! Can't you see that man is injured? Help him on in here by the fire before he drowns in his own duds!"

Clara looked up at Longarm with those liquid cobalt blues of hers that belonged to a much younger girl. "Are you hurt bad, Longarm?"

"Ah, hell," Longarm said, sliding his rifle from its scabbard and hobbling over to the porch steps. "I been cut worse shavin'."

Clara came up beside him, drew his arm around her shoulders, and helped him up the steps and into the major's headquarters office. Colby came in behind them after ordering the corporal to stable the black. Longarm called to the soldier to bring back his grullo with the Three Forks brand on its withers. The major's eyes were fervent as he said, "Did you see her? Did you see Señorita Revenge, and . . . I hope . . . *kill* her?"

Longarm sagged into a chair across from the man's broad desk, which fronted a map of western and southern Texas hanging on the adobe brick wall behind it. There was a monkey stove against the wall on the lawman's right, and he shuddered again as the warmth from its sticks of burning pine reached out to caress him, soft as Señorita Revenge's . . . *er, Valencia Quine's?* . . . breasts.

Even beat up, wounded, exhausted, and soaked, he couldn't get the image of the beautiful savage out of his mind. "I saw her," Longarm said. "She and three others ambushed me. I sent three to their rewards, but when I was getting ready to drill the señorita, she vanished. Like the damn wind or some old Injun spirit." He couldn't help chuckling as Clara, on her knees before him, grunted while she tugged on his boot. "I'm still not entirely sure what I saw was her."

"It was her, all right," Colby said, walking around Longarm to hike a hip on the edge of his desk, his eyes sliding around in their sockets as he pondered the situation. "She's getting braver and braver all the time. She's never actually attacked the outpost till now, only bushwhacked small- to medium-sized patrols. I'm gonna need more men from Fort Stockton or I'm . . . afraid . . ."

"Afraid of what?"

"I'm afraid regimental headquarters will close the outpost here until we can get the situation under control." As Clara pulled Longarm's boot off, nearly falling back against her father's desk as she did, the major fired a hard, commanding look at the federal lawman. "I won't be run out of here with my tail between my legs. Damn it, she must be killed, Longarm! That girl must die. She's the head of that ragtag bunch of Kiowa. We cut the head off, the rest of the snake dies."

"I'm workin' on it."

Longarm winced as Clara, who'd peeled his sock off, now rolled the cuffs of his whipcord trousers up past the bloody hole in his left calf. He turned his head to one side to get a good look at the wound. The bullet had only clipped him, entering on the left rear where his calf bulged the broadest and exiting only a couple of inches over on the other side.

Clara tipped her head to inspect it, and Longarm's toes grazed her breasts sloping out from the men's wool shirt she wore. Clara sucked a sharp breath. "That must hurt, Longarm!"

"It burns some, but it's not as bad as it looks. Probably blew out a thumb-sized chunk of meat, but it'll grow back. I just got to get it sewed up, so I can ride tomorrow. There's a kit in my saddlebags back in the spare room at your house. If you'd admire to fetch it for me, Miss Clara, I'd be forever beholdin'."

"Yes, and bring a bottle of brandy, too—will you, Clara?"

"Of course!" The woman-child fairly leaped to her feet and dashed out of the headquarters door and into the muddy yard.

Colby frowned at Longarm, who found himself staring out the window left of the major's desk while he held his handkerchief taut against his calf, which was now resting atop the other knee. The major glanced out the window himself, rising tensely. "What is it? They're not back, are they?"

"No." Longarm shook his head. "I think you're safe for a couple of days, at least." He looked at the major. "You ever seen Sam Quine's Mexican daughter?"

The major looked incredulous. "Quine's daughter? Not that I remember. I heard he'd adopted a Mex girl when her family was killed on the other side of the border. He and his wife, Elizabeth, couldn't have any of their own. Elizabeth Quine is half-Mexican. Her grandfather fought with Santana at the Alamo, I heard tell."

"That's all you know about the daughter, Valencia?"

"That's her name? Yeah, that's all I know about her. Longarm, you wanna tell me why you're askin' about Sam Quine's adopted Mexican daughter?"

"Maybe later. Just thinkin' things through."

The major strolled over to the open front door through which the refreshingly cool, damp, aromatic air wafted. Only a slight mist fell beyond, the previous rain still dripping off the eaves. The old soldier began packing his pipe as he said in a ruminative tone, "What about my daughter?"

Longarm turned to him. "Say again?"

"What do you think of her?"

Longarm's ears warmed with chagrin, remembering his indiscretion with Clara Colby in the mineral bath. "Very nice gal, Major."

"I can see she's quite smitten with you."

"Well, like I said—she's a very nice gal. Surprised she ain't married yet."

"Yes, well . . . there have been . . . uh . . . complications in that regard." The major continued to slowly pack his pipe.

"Oh?" Longarm had an idea that the girl's sanity or lack thereof might at least be one of those complications. Did the major have any idea that her honor might be less than unblemished?

"She needs a home away from here. A good life with a good man. One who's not a career soldier. I brought her out here because she's a delicate creature, and I felt I needed to keep an eye on her. Which I do . . . until she finds someone who can take over for me."

"What're you sayin', Major?" Longarm snorted his disbelief. "You ain't tryin' to marry her off, are you? To *me?*"

The major glanced over his shoulder at him, holding

his meerschaum in one hand, an unlit match in the other. "I'm not getting any younger. And I've forbidden her to get too closely acquainted with any of my men. That's limited her opportunities a great deal. You seem a good man to me, Longarm. And Clara's a good girl. She'd be even better with a husband, maybe a house and a couple of kids. That's the kind of girl she is, just like her mother was."

Longarm couldn't quite work his mind around what the major was saying. He vaguely wondered if he hadn't lost too much blood. Or maybe his brains were scrambled worse than he'd thought they were. But, more likely, the major's own brains were scrambled. He'd seen it in the man's eyes the first time he'd met him.

"Major, I'll be damn lucky to make it out of Texas alive. Now, if I somehow find a way, without bein' killed by that feral Kiowa gal . . ."

"I have the utmost confidence in your abilities, Marshal Long. You're boss, Chief Marshal Vail, assured me you were an excellent tracker and shooter. With such pronouncements, I'm certain you're the man who can track her to her lair, where she'll least expect to be found, and drill a bullet through her savage heart."

"I do appreciate the vote of confidence. But gettin' back to Clara—you'd best get her out of here. And soon. There's a dead brave behind your house, and he was there, I think, to kill your daughter."

The major looked offended. "Why on earth would he want to kill Clara?"

"I don't know. You tell me. But I think Señorita Revenge and the brunt of her gang were trying to distract your soldiers while this man, no doubt a good shot with a bow and arrow, was sent to stick an arrow in Clara's purty heart, quiet-like!" Longarm held the major's stricken gaze. "Why would Señorita Revenge want to single Clara out

like that, Major? Come on—you must have some reason
in mind!"

"How would that savage even know about Clara, unless
she'd been keeping a close scout on the post . . . ?" The
major let his voice trail off darkly, pensively, staring at the
floor as he thought it through.

Clara's voice said, "Did I hear my name?"

The heels of her short boots thudded on the porch, and
then she was standing in the doorway, Longarm's saddlebags hanging over her shoulder, her eyes wide and expect-
ant. She held a bottle down low in her right hand. The
major glanced at Longarm. Hearing the thumps of a
horse's hooves on the soggy ground, Longarm looked out
the window to his left again. The corporal was leading his
saddled grullo up toward the front of the headquarters.

Quickly, Longarm tied the handkerchief around his calf
and used his rifle to help him rise.

"I was just sayin' I sure would like to hang around the
house this evenin', Miss Clara . . ." He took the saddlebags
from her and leaned down to peck her on the cheek. "But
I've decided it might be best for me to go on over to San
Simon, get a doctor to tend this wound, after all. He'll
likely give me somethin' to help me sleep, so I can get up
at the first flush of dawn and get after them Injuns."

Longarm hobbled out to where the corporal was tying
his grullo to the hitchrack. He looked over Cora's head,
giving the major a pointed, commanding look to keep a
sharp eye on his daughter while the Kiowa were still a
threat. The major stared at him blankly, still running
through his crazy, cluttered mind the information that
Clara might have been singled out for assassination by
Señorita Revenge.

The girl, looking innocent but troubled and obviously
still rattled by the arrow that had been flung toward her

earlier, turned toward Longarm as the lawman draped his saddlebags over the grullo's back. "But . . . I don't understand, Longarm. I thought you were going to have supper with Father and me, and, uh . . ." She gave her mouth corners a devilish quirk. "Bed down in our spare room tonight . . . ?"

The corporal, standing at attention beside the porch steps, slid his eyes quickly to Longarm and then aimed them straight out toward the southern horizon, his face an exaggerated blank.

Longarm swung the horse away from the major's headquarters, pinching his hat brim to the girl. "I'll see you again soon, Miss Clara. Major." With that, he booted the grullo along the muddy parade ground, where a soldier was returning the flag to its pole, and on toward San Simon on the other side of the creek.

He'd just thumped across the same bridge he'd taken on his way from town before, when two riders appeared on the muddy trail ahead of him. Longarm reined up the grullo, frowning against the pink glare of the sun angling in under the broken storm clouds to the west and reflecting off the adobe hovels.

One of the approaching riders rode upright while the other rode belly-down across his McClellan saddle. When the upright soldier's eyes found the big man riding toward him, his hand automatically slipped across his belly toward the army-issue Colt positioned for the cross-draw on his left hip.

"At ease, Private," Longarm said with a weary air, glancing at the man, also in cavalry blues, draped across his saddle. A tan kepi was wedged between the man's belly and his saddle.

The man groaned and lifted his head, showing the large numeral eight with the diagonal line cut through it.

Captain Stockley stared at Longarm through crossed eyes, the whites of which were liberally etched in red. He tried to uncross his eyes, and grumbled with the effort, but finally let his head flop down against his saddle stirrup, both hands dangling about a foot above the ground.

Longarm sighed and touched heels to the grullo's flanks, pushing on past the owly-looking soldier-executioner, and on into the town that was darkening now as the sun dropped behind the Chisos Mountains.

Chapter 14

As he rode down the street, noticing a fresh batch of soldier-deputies on patrol with their Spencer repeaters, he also noticed a subdued air. No doubt everyone in the village had heard the rattling of the Gatling gun earlier and was aware that Señorita Revenge had come calling.

The Anglos and Mexicans drinking together on the plazas outside the saloons and cantinas spoke in hushed, grave tones. The shopkeepers swept their boardwalks or moved their merchandise inside with quick, furtive movements, casting cautious glances at Longarm clip-clopping by on Sam Quine's grullo. There was none of the boisterousness and music one would normally hear this late in the day in a mostly Mexican-populated village, when the watering holes would usually be stoking themselves for the night.

When Longarm had first ridden into the town, he'd seen a hotel along a southern side street, a block or so away from the main road. Figuring he'd get a better night's sleep over there than in the heart of the drinking district—the good citizens of San Simon were sure to forget their fears, or at least start drowning them, in an hour or so—he pointed the grullo toward the hotel.

There was a small livery barn behind it, so he stabled the horse there, with the old Mexican proprietor and his shaggy-headed young grandson, both of whom eyed him with puzzling skepticism. Limping, again using his rifle for a crutch, he hauled his saddlebags into the two-story, cracked adobe saloon via a back door and hobbled up to the bar.

Besides the apron—a sallow-faced Anglo in a bow tie and crisp green apron—there were only three other men in the place—two Mexicans and an old Anglo man sitting on a piano bench with his skinny legs crossed. He had a face like a worn-out, old coyote, and he was leisurely smoking a cigarette and nursing a beer.

Longarm leaned against the bar, thoroughly tired of the ache in his leg and the wet clothes still sagging on him and making him feel as though he weighed fifty pounds more than he did. "Room. Some good rye—Tom Moore, if you have it—and food. The room better come with a good stove."

His sodden state and injury had turned his bones to icicles.

The barman scowled at him as he set a key and a bottle on the scarred bar top. He regarded the lawman with much the same look as the pair in the livery stable had, and as the three currently flanking him did.

The barman said in a hoarsey rasp, "There's a key for room twelve. There's a bottle. You won't find Tom Moore within a thousand square smiles. I'll send some chili up when it's done. You're a little early for supper. That will be two dollars and two bits."

"Did I do somethin' to offend you gents?"

The sallow-faced barman blinked slowly and rolled a match from one corner of his mouth to the other. "We sorta figured you was the big federal badge toter that Colby called in to kill Señorita Revenge and her gang of Kiowa cutthroats."

Suddenly, clarity befell Longarm. "Oh, I see. So what am I doin' limpin' in here in this backstreet flophouse when I should be out huntin' her down and putting a bullet in her heart? That it? Or, why the hell haven't I already performed the nasty deed?"

"That's it," said one of the Mexicans—a willowy man with a groomed beard and wearing a three-piece suit. A shopkeeper, most likely.

"Well, I do apologize for my negligence," Longarm said, tossing some gold onto the bar. "But you probably know—since you know who I am, and all—that I only got here just today and that the huntin' down and killin' of a girl, especially one as mean an' nasty as Señorita Revenge, takes a little more time than a couple of hours."

"Why, look at him—he's wounded!" the man sitting on the piano bench said accusingly, pointing his cigarette at Longarm's lower leg.

"Ah, Christ," said the barman. "We're doomed. She's gonna drive everyone out of San Simon before we can open the spring!"

The Mexican gent pounded his fist on his table and lurched to his feet. "I say we tell Colby to put a bounty on her head. It's time for bounty hunters, I say!"

The other Mexican, dressed similarly to the first one and smoking a thick stogie, said, "If the army and the government's heller can't do it, then why not hire bounty hunters? *Sí*—I am all for it!"

Longarm groaned, grabbed his bottle and his key and his rifle, adjusted the saddlebags on his shoulder, and headed up the stairs at the end of the room. He hobbled up to room twelve and went in. Fifteen minutes later he had a fire burning in the sheet-iron stove that sat in a corner near the foot of the bed and below the window, which he'd closed the shutters over. He'd stripped down to his birthday suit and draped his clothes over the bed's brass frame, positioning his boots just far enough away from getting overly hot and stiffening up.

Sitting in a chair within a few feet of the stove, he went to work sewing up the two holes in his calf. He could let them heal on their own, but not without risking them opening up on him again when he hit the trail tomorrow after Señorita Revenge.

The barman brought up a bowl of chili and a bowl of crusty bread, and Longarm paused in his sewing to devour half the chili and the bread before resuming the work of stitching himself up.

He pinched the entrance hole closed with his thumb and index finger and poked the threaded needle into one side of the puck and drew it through to the other. He clenched his jaws and grunted, ground his right heel into the floor. Performing such a maneuver was best left to professionals, but contrary to what he'd told Miss Clara, he didn't want to bother with a bona fide pill roller, especially when he'd had plenty of practice performing such operations on himself in the past.

True, a few times he'd passed out from the pain before the job was finished, but this was a relative bee sting compared to other such perforations he'd endured over the years.

He pulled the thread through tight and, holding the needle up above his leg, reached down, grabbed the bottle of rye—it wasn't Tom Moore, but it would do—and took two deep swallows. Some of the rye leaked out the sides of his mouth and dribbled down his chin. He leaned forward and let the drops land on the wound, which was like touching it with a match flame, but it would kill any infection, and why waste tanglefoot on a dirty floor?

He took one more pull from the bottle, reminding himself not to get too drunk before he'd finished the procedure, then set it back down on the floor. As he poked the needle through the pinched skin on the other side of the entrance wound, he distracted himself with thoughts of Señorita Revenge and Major Colby and the major's comely, albeit crazy, daughter.

He could come to few conclusions about any of them—aside from the most obvious one. As he'd been told by Colby, the crazy Kiowa gal needed killing. He was a lawman, not an assassin, but he saw little way out of killing her. He doubted there would be any sitting down and reasoning with the likes of Señorita Revenge, who was doing a damn good job of embarrassing not only Major Colby but every soldier at Sotol Creek.

If it was up to him, he'd close down the Sotol Creek outpost until the trouble was over. Might save some men that way. But he supposed that would have been all the more embarrassing for Colby and every cavalry soldier in the Big Bend.

Imagine soldiers being run off their post by a woman and a handful of Kiowa braves? If the Eastern newspapers got ahold of the story, the entire U.S. Cavalry would become a laughing stock. That's why Longarm was here. Longarm, the girl killer.

He paused in the sewing of his leg and took another pull from the bottle. The idea still didn't sit right with him. Of course, it probably would have helped if she'd been ugly.

He finished sewing the wound and then gave it a good whiskey bath. That caused him to suck a sharp breath, throwing his head back, the cords in his neck standing out like ropes. Beneath the sucking sound, a squawk sounded from the other side of the door.

He turned to see a shadow beneath the door. The shadow moved first one way and then the other. It grew slightly, as though the person obviously standing on the other side of the door was leaning closer to it. The doorknob twisted slightly from side to side.

Longarm slowly gained his feet, wincing at the pain in his freshly stitched calf, and slid his Colt from its holster. Stealthily, he hobbled over to the door, staying wide of the keyhole in case someone was looking through it, trying to draw a bead on him so they could gun him through the door.

It had been tried before, several times almost successfully.

He pressed his shoulder against the wall left of the door, slipped his pistol into his left hand, and wrapped his hand around the knob. He didn't care that he was naked. When someone was trying to kill you, things like that didn't matter. He twisted the knob until the latch clicked, then drew the door wide, releasing it.

It banged against the wall. A short, dark figure, stood before him. Light from a couple of bracketed hall candles glinted off a gun barrel. There was a gasp—one that was just high-pitched enough for Longarm to not shoot the person holding the gun outside his door, and not even slam his fist into the person's face.

Unconsciously, or maybe because he could smell a feminine fragrance, he knew he was dealing with a female. The girl gasped as he chopped his right hand down on top of the gun. It dropped to the floor with a thud.

She gave a low squeal as he grabbed her by the front of her coat, drew her inside the room, and threw her onto the bed. He threw himself on top of her and found himself staring into the two, savage black eyes of Señorita Revenge.

Or . . . was she Valencia Quine?

"No, please, Marshal Long!" she squealed, crumpling her eyes with what appeared genuine fear. "Don't hurt me!"

Longarm straddled her, grabbed her by the arms, and shook her. "Which one are you?"

"Please! You're hurting me!"

She was, indeed, the spitting image of Señorita Revenge. Only one way to find out . . .

He grabbed the collar of her red, fancily stitched brocade coat, and tore it halfway down her chest. Beneath, she wore a loose silk blouse. As she writhed and squealed under him, he ripped the blouse, too, until her brown breasts lay exposed beneath him.

The skin above the girl's cleavage was smooth as a baby's ass. No tattoo.

"What the hell is goin' on in here?" This from the door, where a middle-aged man in cowboy garb stood glaring. He pointed a finger at Longarm as the big lawman, wearing only the bandage on his calf, was straddling the dark-haired girl on the bed. "Hey, what're you doin' in there, you damn pervert? That girl don't look like she . . ."

The man let his voice trail off as Longarm climbed down off the bed and hobbled toward him. He backed away, eyes raking the big, brawny, naked man before him, and then acquired a sour look and held his hands up, palms out, as though he were afraid he'd be given similar treatment as the girl.

Longarm kicked her pistol into the room, then slammed the door. When he turned to her, she lay on her side on the bed, holding an arm across her breasts. Her gaze dropped to his dong that, of its own accord, had filled out a little at the sight of the girl's tan bosom, and her eyes widened.

"*Christo!*" she cried, clutching her arm tighter across her breasts. "Please don't ravage me!"

Chapter 15

"Why the hell shouldn't I ravage you, Señorita Quine?"

Longarm went over and felt of his longhandles. They were still damp. So he grabbed a towel off a spike driven into the side of the dresser and wrapped it around his waist.

"Usually, when girls show up at my room unannounced, that's what they're lookin' for. Either that or they're lookin' to shoot me, and in that event I feel like they're fair game for anything I got in mind."

He glanced at the .36 Remington that had slid up against a leg of the dresser, before returning his gaze to the girl cowering on the bed.

She swallowed, shook her head. "No. I did not come here to shoot you."

"Don't tell me you were picking your teeth with that popper."

"I was scared. A girl alone amongst men. I was afraid someone would accost me, and I wanted to make sure they knew I wasn't . . . for sale. I figured that if they saw the gun, they'd leave me alone. I was looking for you, Marshal Long, but not to shoot you!"

"You'll forgive me if I remain skeptical until all the evidence is in."

Longarm sagged down onto a hide-bottom chair in a corner near the door, the girl and the bed about six feet away from him. He'd like to have been closer to the stove, but that would have meant being closer to the girl, and he didn't trust himself.

There was just something too damn intoxicating about her—the blue-black hair, the chiseled face with cherry skin on flat cheeks tapering down to a long, narrow jaw. A fine, delicate body with just enough curves to set a man's nerves to sparking.

There was also, undeniably, the slightly uncivilized, rapacious glimmer in the lustrous, chocolate eyes, though that wasn't as pronounced in Valencia Quine's eyes as in those of Señorita Revenge . . .

"You're sisters?" he asked.

She sat up, holding her blouse closed, glancing at him sidelong, eyes flickering shyly across his bare torso. *"Sí."*

"Tell me about it."

She proceeded then, haltingly, to tell about how she and her twin sister, whose Kiowa name was Koma, had been orphaned when a contingent of cavalry had raided their village along the Rio Grande, killing their parents and everyone else living in the small collection of wickiups— young and old and everyone in between, even several babies. Valencia, whose name then was Melah-ni, or "Morning Flower," and Koma had been hidden under a cutbank by their mother.

After the attack, the girls were found wandering alone by Sam Quine, whose ranch lay in the same area along the river. Quine took in both girls, for his wife couldn't bear children of her own, but when young Koma turned out to be too much to handle, and had tried to cut Quine's wife with a butcher knife, he sent her to a convent on the other side of the Rio Grande, in Mexico. The naturally reticent, deferring Melah-ni was much more acceptable to her Anglo father and half-Mexican mother.

The nuns apparently knew just what do with her headstrong, defiant sister, who refused to learn their ways. They held her down and carved the mark of Satan into her chest, just above her flowering bosoms. The line through the S, making it look like an 8, was a talisman recognized by the ancient sect the nuns belonged to—a representation readily identifiable in purgatory, where its bearer wouldn't linger long, or be able to fool her way into heaven, before being cast into the fires of hell.

After suffering the pain and humiliation of the tattoo, Koma escaped from the nuns and joined a small band of especially defiant Kiowa roaming the canyons along the Rio Grande, determined to rid their ancestral lands of the white man's scourge. After a few years, proving herself to be as ruthless, savage, and efficient at killing as any of the bucks, she became their leader.

One of her first triumphs was leading her band of warriors against the convent where she'd been held for almost a year. She crucified all the nuns before burning the place to the ground, and then set her sites on the cavalry captain who'd led the raid on her people's village back when she and her sister were ten.

"Colby," Longarm said, the name popping instantly into his head.

"Sí."

"How did she know, after all that time?"

"She'd been searching for that man, and she saw him from a distance about a year ago when she and her band were scouting the outpost. And she remembered the man with the savage scar across his face, those vacant, evil eyes, the fancy pipe sticking out of his pocket. She bided her time, choosing to make him suffer slowly for his sins, killing only a few of his men at a time, confounding him thoroughly, before . . .'"

"Before she'd kill his daughter, and make him truly suffer. And then, I assume, she'd kill him, too."

"Crucifiy him." Was that a smile quirking the pretty señorita's mouth corners, making copper javelins dance in her dark brown eyes? "*Sí.* But only after she killed every man at the outpost. Only when they ran out of men would she kill this savage *yanqui* killer, Major Colby."

"How did she know the higher-ups wouldn't just close the outpost? It's a small one, after all. Not worth all this trouble."

"Because of the springs."

"The springs." Longarm pondered that, remembering that one of the Mexican businessmen had mentioned a springs downstairs in the hotel's saloon. "You mean, the one behind the major's house."

Valencia nodded. "My father and many of the businessmen around town have talked about it, including Major Colby, of course. It was his idea. From what I've overheard my father saying to my mother, the major has learned that springs are valued by the people back east. They will pay money to come and bathe in them. And the springs in the Big Bend are supposed to be especially beneficial."

"Ah, for health." Longarm smiled in spite of the pain in his raw, freshly sewn leg. "Easterners been coming in droves to several springs in the Rockies. There's been one in northern Colorado—a famous one—for quite some time." He meant the one in the town of Glenwood Springs, in the mountains west of Denver. "So, that's why he's been tryin' so hard to keep the outpost open?"

"*Sí*. He wants to keep it open long enough to tame this country, as well as San Simon, so that the people from the East will come, as you say, in droves. They will pay much money to stay in the hotels and to bathe in the springs."

"But only, of course, if Señorita Revenge has been run to ground, and San Simon has been turned into a nice, quiet, little resort town. Free of the bandito and pistolero element."

"That is what I understand."

Longarm had taken his bottle off the dresser and stood now near the dresser, staring at the small, ticking stove in the corner, thinking it all through. He took a pull from the bottle, looked at the girl. "I'm sorry about you and your sister. I could tell Colby wasn't right in the head. The look in his eyes, the way he runs the town, his daughter. Still, what your sister's been doing—the army won't condone it. It changes nothing. You and her could try to bring charges against Colby, but his raid on your family's village was so long ago . . ."

He let his voice trail off, genuinely feeling sorry for the girl, and about what Colby's actions had caused to happen to her sister, not to mention to the major's own men. Unfortunately, such evil doings were all too common in the frontier army.

It was still Longarm's duty to put a stop to Señorita Revenge's depredations. The assignment had sickened him before. Now it made him sicker. He took another pull from the bottle, to quell the snakes stirring around in his belly. The whiskey didn't accomplish its intent. Longarm set the bottle on the dresser and sat on the bed beside Valencia, who sat as before, ankles crossed, head down, arms crossed on her torn coat and shirt.

"I do apologize for treating you so roughly, Miss Valencia. You didn't deserve that, especially in light of all you been through."

She sniffed, and only then did he realize she was sobbing. She wiped a tear from her cheek with the back of her hand and shook her hair back from her face. "I came here with my gun out. And of course I look like my sister. You would have been a fool to do otherwise."

"Surely your parents don't know you're here."

"I saddled a horse and stole away from the rancho early this morning. It's twenty miles south of San Simon. I knew you'd been sent to kill my sister, and I had to tell you what I just told you. You must know."

"You must know it doesn't really change much, except the fact that I'd like to put a bullet in Colby. Before I leave here, he'll know I intend to file a report with my boss in Denver, who will make sure it gets shown around the War Department in Washington." Longarm shook his head. "Otherwise, I still gotta stop your sister. She's murdering innocent men."

"*Sí.*" Valencia looked up at him. "I know she must be stopped. I just wanted you to know what caused all the trouble in the first place."

"How do you two stay in touch?"

"We meet occasionally. Where, I can't tell you. We also send signals using mirrors."

Longarm nodded his understanding. "She is your blood, after all." He withdrew his arm from her shoulders. "You'd best get a room, señorita. Your horse must be blown. You'll both need a night's rest before you head back to your ranch."

"My horse is stabled with yours. I saw you when you rode in from the outpost, and followed you here. I have no money for a room."

"I have money. I'll go down and arrange for—"

She threw her arms around him, buried her face in his chest. "I will stay here with you."

"No, no, no." He tried to shove her away, but she only clung to him more tightly. Her body was supple against his, her breath warm and moist as it fluttered against his breastbone.

"I feel safe here, with you. After all, you saved my life once. I will sleep here, in your bed."

"That's out of the question."

She drew away from him, shrugged out of her coat, tossed it onto the floor, and let her loose blouse and chemise tumble off her shoulders, exposing her firm, uptilted breasts. Her dark eyes held his. "Is it?"

"Ah, hell. Don't do that." Longarm tried to lift her blouse back up over her breasts, but she threw herself against him, rose up on her knees, wrapped her arms around his neck, and kissed him hungrily. Her tongue slipped into his mouth and pressed against his as she mashed her lips harder against his own.

"You are a man," she breathed, her lips barely touching his, mashing her breasts against his naked chest. "I am a woman. My father keeps a tight rein on me, but I am twenty years old, Longarm." She groaned and kissed him, pulled her mouth away as she ran her hands across his back, pressing the heels of her hands against his shoulder blades. "I have never been fucked, and as Koma tells me, I can never be a woman until I have had a hard cock between my legs!"

Longarm jerked his head back, surprised and amazed by the sudden burst of farm talk from the formerly shy, reticent child. He didn't know what to say. He felt his cock stir under the towel he wore around his waist. She smiled, reached under the towel, and found him.

Her smile grew, copper chips glinting in her eyes.

"Christos!" she breathed. "I have never seen one except on horses. Can I see it?"

"Damn it, Valencia, my leg's all shot up. I need another drink and some sleep. Got a long ride ahead . . ."

He let his voice trail off as her hand massaged him under the towel, and he felt his cock growing, hardening of its own accord. The rawness and pain in his calf subsided beneath the tingling in his nether regions. How was a man supposed to deny such a delectable little filly as the one who sat beside him now, squeezing her eyes closed and making little mewling noises as she pumped his cock?

Her dark breasts jostled beneath the messy screen of her coarse, black hair. Suddenly, he found himself cupping the young orbs in his hands, flicking his thumbs across the pebbled nipples, causing them to distend like they'd done in the dream he'd had of her back on the shore of the Rio Grande.

She continued to massage him, pump him hungrily, running her small hand all over his now fully erect appendage.

"I want to see it," she whispered.

Longarm stood and dropped the towel. She stared at it, jaw falling, eyes widening. She sat back on her outstretched arms and chuckled.

"Now, Miss Valencia," he said, "laughing at a naked man is no way to start things off."

"It's so big!" She leaned forward, cupped his balls gently in one hand, wrapping her other hand around the base of the shaft. "Are they all like that?"

"Same basic design, I reckon," he said with a growl, his pulse hammering in his temples. "Size differs from man to man."

"This one looks like some I've seen on my father's stud horses." She looked up at him from beneath her brows and then stuck her tongue out, keeping her eyes on his, as though she were doing something she dared him to stop. She touched her tongue to the tip of his cock, running it slowly, gently up and down the tip for a time before tracing the entire mushroom head.

He groaned as she closed her mouth over it and began to suck him, making wet sounds and caressing his balls with her left hand, keeping the right one planted firmly around the shaft. Each of her cheeks bulged in turn as she shifted the head around inside of her mouth. Her bare breasts looked exactly as they'd looked in his dream, and now they sloped slightly out from her chest, behind the thin curtain of her long, black hair, the nipples hard and distended.

Longarm stepped back from her, pulling his cock out of her mouth. He pushed her back onto the bed, sat down beside her, and began to undress her. He removed her skirt and then her pantaloons and the garter belts that held up her long, black, silk stockings. He slid the stockings down her long, brown legs and long, slender feet, and dropped them on the floor.

Naked and suddenly shy, she shrank back from him, gazing at him coyly and raising her knees toward her belly. Between her thighs, he saw the little dark patch of hair encircling the pink folds of her snatch. He took both her feet in his hands and used them to spread her knees as he lowered his head to her pussy and pushed his face against it.

He caressed her with his nose and his mustache. She whimpered and grunted and sighed, jerking involuntarily, arching her back. He stuck his tongue between those pink, petal-like folds, and when he could tell he'd brought her near the portal of her climax, he stopped.

"*Mierda!*" she hissed with surprising savageness,

gritting her teeth and looking down at him. Her eyes sparked with unbridled lust and passion, demanding he continue.

"Hold on."

Longarm snaked his arms beneath the girl and lay her lengthways on the bed. Keeping her knees spread with his hands, he lowered himself on top of her, kissed her nose, her cheeks, her lips. He nuzzled her neck for a time, and she hugged him tightly, cooing, shivering, gently flapping her knees in desperation for what was to come.

He suckled her breasts and then slid his tongue slowly down from between the firm mounds to her belly button. And then he lifted his head and smiled at her, breathing hard, every nerve in his body firing his passion.

"Take it in your hand," he whispered, smoothing her hair back from her cheeks with his hand. "Guide me into you."

She was sweating, panting, gasping. Her eyes glazed with desperation, she looked down between their bellies, closed her hand over his rock-hard cock, and slipped its head into her pussy.

Instantly, he felt the hot, honey-like slickness. She gave a guttural groan, which aroused him even further, as he very slowly pushed his hips closer to hers, sliding his cock deeper and deeper inside her virgin snatch. He had to stop often, to give her womb time to relax and accept him, and when he'd pushed halfway into her, he felt the warmth of her blood flow over him.

She cried out, arching her back, digging her fingers into the sheets on either side of her. She panted as though she were in labor.

"Stop?" he asked.

"Uhn-*UHH!*" Then she reached around him, pressed her hands into his buttocks, and pulled him down harder, until he was entirely inside her and pumping away, causing the bedsprings to kick up a raucous rhythm and the headboard to hammer against the wall.

When he came, the knowledge that she'd given up her virginity to him made the spasms all the more violent. He groaned as he bucked against her, Valencia thrusting her pelvis against his, laughing now, singing in Spanish, and then laughing some more and cursing like a wild-assed vaquero on a Friday night in Durango.

"Oh, Christ!" He stopped thrusting, spent, and leaned down to press his cheek against hers, wrapping his left arm around her head.

She was hot and sweaty beneath him. Their groins were stuck together from the mixing of their bodily fluids.

"Regrets?" he asked, knowing it was always possible after the girl's first time.

She raked a hand through his hair, caressed his ass with the heel of her left foot. "If I'd known how wonderful it was, I would have listened to Koma and done it a long time ago."

She chuckled and ground both heels into his ass. "I'm glad the first time was with you, though. My only sadness is that I'll never find another stud horse like you, Longarm!"

He chuckled as he rolled off of her. He rose a little unsteadily from the bed. The whiskey had quelled the ache in his calf, but the frantic tussling had started it hollering again, so he took a long pull from the bottle. Then, while he shared his chili with her, and even a few sips of his whiskey, he warmed some water on the stove.

When the water was steaming, he washed them both, while she kissed him tenderly, nuzzling his neck, running her silky fingers down along his thighs, occasionally letting them brush his flaccid member and flick across his balls.

"*Mierda*, I do have one regret," she said, when he'd emptied the pink water into the porcelain chamber pot and set the pot by the door.

"What's that?" He'd just turned back to her when he saw her gun come up from behind her. The revolver looked as large as a Buntline special in her small hands. There was a click as she drew the hammer back.

"That I'm going to have to kill you now."

Chapter 16

Longarm looked from the gun's dark, round maw to the girl's dark, round eyes above it. The pistol shook in her hands. Her eyes glistened. Tears oozed out of their corners and dribbled down her cheeks.

"I'm sorry, Longarm."

"Ah, hell, I know," Longarm said. "She's your blood. You'd do anything at any cost to save her." He walked toward the bed, limping on his bad leg. "Even if it means drilling a hole through the heart of a man you just slept with."

Valencia tried to harden her jaws, but she only sobbed, and more tears dribbled down her cherry-tan cheeks. Her breasts quivered, the ends of her hair dancing along their sides. "I didn't come here to kill you. Only to make you see that none of this is her fault. But now I realize that there's nothing I can do to stop you, so I *must* shoot you, Longarm. I must!"

He sat down on the edge of the bed, reached out, and took the gun from her hands. It came away easily. "I know you must, but you just can't. See, now? It isn't in you. You wish it was. You wish you were more like her. But you just ain't."

He depressed the hammer and set the gun down on the bed beside him. She fell against his chest, wrapping her arms around him and sobbing with abandon, soaking his chest and belly with her tears. She fell asleep after a time, and then he banked the fire against the chilly night, and lay back in the bed, the girl curled beside him, breathing softly, regularly. He covered them both with the blankets, and he lay there for a time, drinking the whiskey to kill the pain in his calf and smoking a cheroot, blowing the smoke out through the darkness toward the door.

Finally, the whiskey and exhaustion burrowing through the pain, he turned the lamp down on the bedside table and went to sleep. Someone rapped on the door. He jerked his head up, heart thudding, hand reaching for his Colt as Valencia lifted her head with a gasp. He looked at the door touched with the salmon rays of the morning sun pushing between the cracks in the shuttered window.

The rap came again. A familiar voice said, "Marshal Long?"

"What the hell . . . ?"

"It's Captain Stockley. Trouble out at the post. Señorita Revenge slipped into the major's house last night and took Miss Colby."

Longarm shoved his revolver back down in the holster hanging off the bedpost and glanced at Valencia. She stared worriedly toward the door, holding the blankets over her breasts. Her hair was badly tangled.

"Koma," she said in a dark, fateful voice.

"You stay here," Longarm said softly. Then, rising, he said louder, "I'll be out in a minute, Captain."

Out in the hall, boots thudded, dwindling into the

distance. They clomped off down the stairs. Longarm picked up his longhandles, wincing at the pain in his calf, his mind racing over what he'd just learned from Stockley.

Clara taken by Señorita Revenge. He could imagine the girl's horror, her darkest dreams coming true. She must be near death with terror.

"Miss Colby?" Valencia said. "She is . . ."

"Major Colby's daughter. Your sister tried to kill her yesterday. Must've decided to try another tactic last night, circling around back to the outpost. Gotta hand it to her, she sure as hell does the unexpected."

"She took Miss Colby because she knows you'll try to get her back. She'll be leading you into a trap."

Longarm had pulled on his dry longhandles. Now he looked at Valencia. "What's wrong with that? Maybe she can accomplish what you couldn't last night."

Valencia leaned toward him, the blankets falling to her lap. "Take me with you?"

Longarm continued quickly dressing. He needed to get after Señorita Revenge, get Clara back home and safe with her father. "Don't be crazy."

"I know where she is going. I know where she always goes." Valencia paused, dropping her eyes, as though reconsidering. But then she lifted them again, and they were touched with resolve. "I am the only one. I can take you to her, Custis."

"Why?" he said, cautious.

"Because it's time for the killing to stop."

She held his befuddled gaze as he continued to dress. "You can trust me." She crawled naked out of bed, picked up her pistol, swept her hair back from her face, and held out the gun to him. "You can keep this."

He stopped buttoning his shirt to take the pistol from

her, hefted it in his hand, pondering it, pondering its owner, then gave it back to her. "No need. Get dressed. I'll go out and saddle our horses."

"Hair of the dog?" he said, when, clomping downstairs into the saloon's main drinking hall, he saw Stockley standing at the bar, one boot propped on the brass rail running along the bottom.

The captain was the only customer. The bartender was nowhere to be seen. Chairs were overturned on tabletops. The place smelled of the sawdust that had been sprinkled on the floor for sweeping. Shadows were thick and spangled with sunlight angling through the front windows.

Before Stockley could answer, Longarm turned at the bottom of the stairs and headed for the back door, only favoring his left leg slightly now after the shot of liquor he himself had enjoyed before leaving his room. Stockley threw back the last of his whiskey shot, grabbed his hat off the bar top, and followed Longarm out of the saloon.

"What happened?" the lawman asked, as he walked toward the livery barn standing between two cottonwoods whose leaves the sun touched with gold.

"She and two others, judging by the tracks, slipped in unseen and unheard, killed the three guards the major had posted around his house. The Kiowa did nothing to the major himself, left him asleep in his room."

Longarm approached the barn, limping only slightly, jaws set grimly. "When did he realize she was gone?"

"Not until he got up at six and found her room empty. No sign of a struggle, but all three guards had been gutted and left lying where they'd been standing."

Longarm swung the barn doors wide and walked into the shadows rife with the smell of hay and ammonia, looking for his and Valencia's horses. "Where's the major now?"

"He headed out with six of our best remaining soldiers about an hour ago. He sent me to fetch you, wants us to rendevous along the trail aways."

"He's tracking them, I take it?"

"Yep, they left tracks in the mud."

"I suggest you don't trust the tracks, Captain," Valencia said, walking toward the barn from the rear of the saloon, taking long strides, hair dancing beneath her small, green felt hat. She'd tied her blouse closed beneath her coat, which was also missing buttons, but the buttons Longarm had ripped off her blouse exposed a good bit of cleavage, her breasts bouncing saucily.

Longarm was walking his grullo out of its stall. Stockley stood staring, hang-jawed, at the Mexican girl walking toward him. A Mexican girl with Indian-dark features, who looked the spitting image of the savage Kiowa princess who'd carved the grisly tattoo into his forehead.

Stockley tensed, closing his fingers around the walnut grips of his Colt .44.

"At ease, Captain. Meet Señorita Valencia Quine. Señorita, meet Captain Stockley."

Valencia paused just inside the doors, parting her lips as she stared at the man in shock. She easily recognized the scar similar to the one her sister wore above her bosoms.

"*Dios mío!*" she said, softly, tonelessly.

Stockley kept his hand around his holstered revolver's butt. "I don't . . . understand."

"She's Señorita Revenge's sister. Told me quite a story last night."

"What story?"

"Later," Longarm said, leading Valencia's fine palomino

mare out of its stall. To the girl, he said, "You say not to trust the tracks she left last night . . . ?"

"She'll only run you into an ambush, or lead you in circles, like rabbits chased by coyotes," Valencia said, retrieving her saddle from a stall partition. It was a regular stock saddle, not a sidesaddle as Longarm would have expected. "I know where she's headed."

"You're Sam Quine's daughter?" Stockley asked, still staring at the girl aghast, though he'd removed his hand from his gun.

"Why don't you fetch your horse, Captain?" Longarm was saddling the grullo. "We'll fill you in on the trail."

"We? You can't mean she's riding *with us?*"

"Makes sense to me, since Valencia knows where her sister's headed."

Stockley continued to stare dubiously at Valencia, who was busy saddling her palomino, and then he swung around and headed out through the barn doors. Longarm tossed his saddlebags over the grullo's back and looked across his saddle at the girl. "She's holed up in the Chisos, isn't she?"

"Sí." Valencia nodded, then crouched behind the palomino as she tightened the latigo. "But you'll never find her hideout without me. No one would."

Longarm slipped his rifle into his saddle boot, his brows bunched in grave thought. He doubted he'd ever see Clara alive again. Likely the major was wolf bait, as well, if Longarm didn't catch up to him and divert him from the trap that Señorita Revenge, or Koma, was likely luring him into, with his daughter the bait there. The lawman hoped he could catch up to the major before the trap was sprung.

Not that he really cared all that much about what happened to Colby. Only the innocent soldiers in his charge and Clara.

When he and Valencia had finished rigging their horses, they rode away from the barn, finding Captain Stockley waiting for them where the side street and the main street intersected. It was still early, with only a few dogs out, a couple of hungry coyotes scavenging in an alley between a little Mexican eatery and a large, frame mercantile owned by one Norbert J. Davis. Stockley led Longarm and Valencia west of town and along the perimeter of the outpost, where the soldiers were on high alert and standing watch with carbines along the creek. Their yellow neckerchiefs, bright in the intensifying sunshine, and the brims of their kepis fluttered in the morning wind.

When they'd cut the trail that the Kiowa party had made early that morning, when the Indians were leaving the fort, ostensibly with Clara, as well as the prints of the major's party who'd lit out after them, Longarm said, "We'll follow the trail till we catch up with Colby. He's probably aware he's being led into an ambush, but with his daughter's life at stake, he might get careless."

"What'll we do after we catch up to him?" Stockley said.

"We'll abandon the señorita's trail and try to cut her off before she reaches her hideout."

Stockley glanced at Valencia, his eyes dark, as though he were looking at the girl who'd so severely branded him. "How do you know you can trust her, Marshal Long? Just because you slept with her last night?" He spat that last out with bitter sarcasm. "She might have seduced you into a trap similar to the one her sister's setting for Colby."

Longarm looked at Valencia, who said nothing. The nubs of her cherry cheeks were touched with red.

"Maybe," Longarm said, reining his horse around and booting it on up the trail through the desert. "I reckon we'll have to take our chances, Captain!"

Chapter 17

An hour later, among the corduroy troughs and ridges spilling down out of the Chisos Mountains, Longarm drew back on the grullo's reins. He lifted his chin and loosened his jaws, listening.

The sound he'd heard came again. A flat *pop*, distantly echoing. There was another and another. The racket continued, as though there were a Fourth of July rodeo ahead, complete with Mexican fireworks, and beneath the cracks and pops of what could only be pistols and carbines, men screamed shrilly.

There were a few shouts. But mostly screams.

"Oh, Lord, no," Stockley said as he reined his army bay to a halt on Longarm's right, squinting through the tan dust rising around them.

Valencia drew her own horse up on Longarm's left. "She found them," she said, fatefully, almost wistfully, staring ahead, long, black hair hanging down her slender shoulders clad in the dusty, cream-white blouse. "They walked into her trap for them."

"Shit!"

Longarm whipped the end of his reins against the grullo's withers. The horse lunged into a ground-chewing gallop. He sped up over a low rise and down the other side. Beyond, in a maze of stony arroyos, he could see figures jostling, smoke rising amid the pops and belches of gunfire. He dropped down into an arroyo, and the grullo galloped along the sandy bottom, following its twisting course southward.

Gradually, the shooting dwindled, before an eerie silence lifted.

Fifteen minutes later, Longarm saw a horse and rider lying on the bottom of where the wash widened between jutting, chalky walls bristling with cactus. He jerked back on the reins. The grullo skidded to a dusty halt, curveting, as Longarm dragged his rifle out of its boot and cocked it one-handed while he leaped to the ground. He'd forgotten his wounded calf, and he raked a sharp breath in now as the pain shot up his leg.

Ignoring it, he strode forward, dropped to a knee beside the dead soldier—a red-haired private—and the dead horse, both pierced with arrows, both with their glassy eyes open in death. As Stockley and Valencia reined up behind Longarm, the lawman straightened and began walking forward along the curving wash.

When he'd rounded a thumb of rock in the gully wall, he saw several more soldiers lying in bloody blue piles before him—stretching away for sixty yards or more. There were two more dead horses amid the dead men, one lying atop a beefy, middle-aged gent with a lance corporal's stripes on his sleeves. Most of Colby's small, remote outpost had been comprised of young men fresh from Jefferson Barracks and older men who'd stayed in the army because they had nowhere else to go, which, coupled with a mad commanding officer, made them all easy pickings for Señorita Revenge.

Holding his rifle high across his chest, Longarm walked up the draw, turning his head from left to right, looking around for the Kiowa. They were most likely gone, but he wasn't taking any chances.

When he came to the last dead soldier, he lowered his rifle slightly and looked back the way he'd come. Valencia and Stockley were walking slowly toward him, the captain holding the stock plate of his Spencer repeater snugged against his shoulder, aiming down the barrel, swinging the gun from one bank to the other, ready for another ambush. His eyes above his brown, dragoon-style mustache were wide and bright with fear.

Valencia stopped and stared at Longarm. She looked pale beneath her natural tan. For a moment, Longarm thought her knees would buckle. He started to move toward her, but she held her hands up, palms out, halting him. She swung around and strode quickly back toward the horses, holding one arm over her belly.

Stockly glanced at her as she passed him, then continued walking toward Longarm. "Doesn't have the stomach for her sister's handiwork, eh?" He stopped beside Longarm, a dark question in his eyes. "Where's Colby?"

"Must've taken him."

"Why?"

Longarm shook his head, then gingerly climbed the bank on his right, looking around the broken, boulder-strewn, cactus-stippled desert rolling up toward the first front of the Chisos Mountains. Ahead, a mare's tail of dust rose, dwindling into the distance and then disappearing altogether as the riders rode behind a jutting wall of sandstone.

Señorita Revenge was gone, heading for her stronghold with, apparently, both Major Colby and Clara. When Longarm was relatively sure that she'd taken her entire war party with her, and hadn't left some to ambush anyone following Colby, he and Stockley returned to where Valencia sat on a rock, shaded by the arroyo wall, waving her hat in her face for air.

"No stomach for your sister's atrocities, Miss Quine?" Stockley asked.

"Shut up, Captain." Longarm set his rifle barrel on his shoulder and looked at Valencia. Her eyes were sad, wounded. "She has Major Colby and his daughter. Why not just kill them?" He thought he knew the answer, but he wanted to hear it from Valencia, who would know better than anyone.

"She wants to torture them slowly. In front of each other. She'll probably kill the girl first, when she's ready to kill her father."

Stockley gave a belligerent chuff.

"Why shouldn't she want to do those things?" Valencia said, regarding Stockley and hardening her voice as well as her eyes. "After what he did to our family? Do you think he deserves any better?"

"The girl is innocent," the captain said with a self-righteous air, dabbing at the scar on his forehead with a white handkerchief.

Valencia wrinkled her slender nose. "So were we, Captain."

Stockley's cheeks flushed with chagrin. He turned to Longarm. "We'd best head back to the outpost. There's nothing more we can do here. Colby's a goner and so is his daughter. I'm the next officer in line, and I'm going to recommend to Fort Stockton that they close the Sotol Creek outpost until Señorita Revenge has been killed or confined to a deep, dark dungeon, shackled, for the rest of her life."

"You two go on back," Longarm said, staring up the

arroyo strewn with dead men, splattered with blood, in the direction in which he'd seen the dust rising. "I'm going to follow her, try to get the Colbys back."

"And kill my sister?"

Longarm looked at Valencia and said none too gently, "Yes."

Valencia blinked slowly. "You won't be able to accomplish that task without me, Custis. It's time for the killing to stop. The only way for that to happen is for Koma to die. I'd like to be there when she dies. I can show you a route to her hideout. We mustn't follow the route she's taking now, because she will eventually plant guards on it, to detour anyone she thinks might be tracking her. I know another way. It's a little longer—it intersects with a trail from the Quine rancho—but it will get us there without her knowing."

"Ah, shit," Colby said, laughing without mirth, looking at Longarm as he held his arm out to indicate Valencia. "She'll run you right into a trap. She's the girl's twin sister, after all." He added through gritted teeth: "And she's *Kiowa*."

Longarm slid his rifle into his saddle boot and said to Stockley, "Head on back to the outpost. If I'm not back in two days, abandon the fort and tell the commander at Fort Stockton he's going to need a couple of brigades to take down Señorita Revenge."

"You're not really riding on!"

"Mount up and ride out, Captain." Longarm looked at him, touching his gaze with understanding. "After what you've been through, there's no shame in it."

He helped Valencia onto her palomino's back and then stepped up into his own saddle. Stockton stood staring at him sidelong, nibbling his mustache, his Spencer angling up from his right hip.

Finally, he said, "Ah, hell!" And he mounted his own horse and looked at Longarm. "We all gotta die sometime. Why not now, at the hands of the Kiowa?"

"Your call, Captain."

Longarm turned to Valencia. "I reckon we'll follow you."

She swung her horse around and booted it back the way they'd come. When the southern slope dropped down considerably, she rode up out of it, and Longarm put the grullo up the bank after her, Stockley following only a few feet behind. Soon they were riding up a steep bench toward a towering cliff. When they reached the cliff, they rested and watered their horses at a stone bowl filled with rainwater, taking a break from the unrelenting sun in a slice of shade angling out from the ridge.

Mounting up again, they continued along a canyon that spilled down out of the higher reaches of the Chisos. Boulders of all shapes and sizes choked the arroyo in places, as did driftwood and pine trees that storm floods had ripped out of the higher moutainside. There was still some water from yesterday's storm, and it was good to have it, as it was a hard ride through rugged country, with few springs.

Cliffs and fingers of rock jutted against the sky. Cedars grew, as did some scraggly sage, but mostly there was only rock and clay dust and gravel. The only wildlife that Longarm saw was a couple of scraggly coyotes digging for a rabbit or a kangaroo rat near a boulder snag.

In the mid-afternoon they rode along a shallow trough through a broad valley sheathed in craggy ridges. There were patches of green grass here, and green shrubs, and Longarm saw some deer and elk droppings, even the tracks of a bear. As the trough rose toward a notch in the ridge ahead of them, Valencia drew rein suddenly, sucking in a sharp breath as she stared straight out in front of her.

Longarm booted his horse up around her, sliding his rifle from its scabbard. "What is it?"

She said nothing but only stared down at two bleached skeletons swathed in ragged, light blue trousers with a yellow stripe running down the outside of the legs. The dead men wore dark blue army tunics, one with a corporal's stripes, the other with a private's, and they lay twisted near the dessicated carcasses of two horses still wearing their saddles.

They were bristling with arrows, at least five apiece. One arrow jutted from an empty eye socket in one of the skulls.

"Probably Max Roberts's party," Stockley said in disgust. "Colby sent the group of nine up here a little over two months ago, bound and determined to find the señorita's lair, while he sent another party south toward Mexico. Neither returned. Those boots there belonged to Private Brian Waters."

He nodded to indicate the boots on the skeleton to the right, non-issue cowboy boots with red stitching in the uppers and with copper spurs. "Regulations are a little looser out here, and, damn, Waters sure loved those boots."

Longarm stared at the boots, and then at the rest of the skeleton to which only a few strips of jerked hide hung in tatters. He gave an inward shudder when he thought about what Clara Colby might be going through at the hands of Señorita Revenge at this very moment.

"Come on," he said, and booted the grullo on up the trough, toward the steep pass jutting like a whipsaw blade ahead.

Shadows were long, the sun about to set, when they reined up at the mouth of another canyon—this one resembling a deep, narrow tunnel showing in the face of solid rock.

"This is where we must be very careful," Valencia said. "Koma might have posted guards in this chasm. On the other end of it is her lair, in a boom town left by Anglos."

"Didn't know there was a town way out here." Stockley scowled at the señorita. "You sure?"

"Don't sell your people short," Valencia said, curling her upper lip. "Your people are as prolific as rabbits." She touched heels to her palomino's flanks and entered the cool, dark mouth of the cavern.

As Longarm followed, the clacks of his horse's hooves echoed off the walls around him. The air grew dank, humid, wonderfully cool against his sweaty, dust-crusted cheeks. There must be a spring-fed stream running along one of the canyon walls, he thought. He could smell a touch of green, like rich, verdant grass. With the water and the country's general ruggedness, it would be a good place for Señorita Revenge's party of Kiowa to hole up, without much chance of being found.

Looking up, Longarm saw a narrow strip of soft, lilac sky between the pale, towering ridges of limestone and sandstone. Birds chirped and piped, their calls echoing richly.

Longarm rode up beside Valencia. He and the girl must have seen the dark-skinned, full-busted specter sitting on the rock ahead of them at the same time, because simultaneously they jerked back on their horses' reins. Behind them they heard a crunching thud and a grunt.

Longarm stared at Señorita Revenge sitting atop a flat boulder just ahead and on the right side of the narrow trail. She leaned forward slightly, bunching her breasts behind the thin, deerskin vest, a shaft of sunlight playing across the scar above the dark cleavage. She kicked her moccasin-clad feet eagerly against the side of the boulder beneath her and smiled, slitting her eyes devilishly.

"Hola, Melah-ni! I see you've brought your wild sister some fresh meat!"

She laughed raucously.

Hooves clomped behind Longarm, who turned to see Stockley's horse moving toward him, looking spooked. The captain sat rigidly, a befuddled look on his pale face. Something protruded from his chest. Blood stained his blue shirt around it. With a deep sigh, he fell forward across his saddle horn.

The wooden shaft of a fletched arrow poked up from the dead center of his back.

"*Sí, mi hermana!*" Valencia said, throwing an eager arm out toward the federal badge toter. "But this lawman called Longarm is enough man for both of us! I was going to kill him last night on your behalf, but he satisfied me so well that I decided to share him with you!"

She held a hand out in front of her crotch, as though hefting something large, and laughed as raucously as her savage sister did.

Chapter 18

Longarm stared at the two girls laughing at him, their chocolate eyes flashing jeers. Stockley's horse nudged Longarm's as it stepped up beside him and then turned, and the captain rolled down the side of his saddle to hit the ground with a solid thump, breaking the arrow protruding from his back.

The man stared up at Longarm, eyes blinking rapidly as they turned opaque, and then he heaved a long last sigh and died.

Longarm slid his hand across his belly toward his Colt. The sudden silence as both girls stopped laughing held his hand. Then he heard the creak of arrow sinew and looked around to see several brown men in the rocks on either side of the trail, aiming nocked arrows at him. They were all armed with rifles, as well—the carbines they'd taken off the soldiers they'd slaughtered over the past several months. The Spencers hung down their backs by leather lanyards. Obviously, maybe because arrows were easier to come by than .56-caliber cartridges, they preferred their more traditional fighting implements.

Señorita Revenge had a carbine, too, as well as a big
bowie sheathed on her shapely thigh and revealed by the
short skirt slitted nearly to her waist on both sides.

"Leave your guns alone, wild man," said Señorita
Revenge, narrowing her eyes at Longarm. "I'd hate to have
to kill a man like you—one who performed so well yesterday even with a bullet hole in his leg."

"You must see how well he performs in bed . . . even
with a bullet hole in his leg." Valencia laughed huskily,
and Longarm's shock only deepened. How could he have
been so badly duped?

"It was about time you learned the pleasures of the flesh,
mi hermana." She started climbing down the side of the
boulder she was on, moving with the grace of a panther
and grinning over her shoulder as she regarded Longarm
lustily. "And what a fine man to start with."

"*Sí*," said Valencia, rubbing her belly and regarding the
lawman with the same expression as her sister. "He cored
me like an apple!" Valencia slid her .36 Remington from
the small holster on her left hip and aimed it at Longarm.
"Toss your guns down, Custis. The Colt and the rifle . . .
and the little double-barreled derringer you wear in your
vest."

"He is well armed, eh?" asked Señorita Revenge as she
dropped to the ground in a crouch.

"*Very* well armed, *mi hermana*." Again, Melah-ni
laughed huskily.

Señorita Revenge walked toward her sister and Longarm, smiling, showing her white teeth between her rich,
pink lips. "I will see for myself soon. As you can see"—
she threw out her arm and open hand to indicate the half
dozen Kiowa warriors, mostly young and old men—men
probably in their forties and fifties, which was old in Indian
years—standing in a nearly complete circle around them,

aiming their bows at Longarm—"I am left with the dregs of my command, due in no small part to your fighting skills, lover." She blinked at Longarm, who tossed his Colt onto the ground near the Kiowa leader's moccasin-clad feet. "You left me with only boys and old men, from whom I receive little satisfaction."

One of the older men took umbrage at that. He lowered his bow and arrow and leaped down out of the rocks—a stocky, muscular gent with many knife scars and a soft belly. His coarse, long hair owned a single, rather thick streak of silver. His broad face was craggy. Longarm thought he was probably only in his thirties, though the hard life of the Kiowa made him look fifty.

He stood before Señorita Revenge, leaning forward and grunting out his guttural tongue, voice pitched with anger, black eyes hard and mean. The señorita gave it back as good as she got, and the man stiffened. He glanced at Longarm, wrinkling his broad, pitted nostrils, and then turned and walked out of the cave.

To Longarm, Señorita Revenge said, "You're a lawman?"

"That's right."

"You must have handcuffs then. Put them on."

"Fresh out," Longarm said, chagrin and fury boiling in him.

"He has some," Valencia said. "I've seen them."

The two stared at him, brows arched.

Longarm sighed, reached back into his saddlebag pouch, and withdrew his handcuffs. He looked around. Five Kiowa warriors were still glaring at him along their nocked bows, waiting for any reason to cut loose on him. They were all jealous of the attention he was being given by the two beautiful women, which put him in a very bad place indeed.

He cuffed himself and then sat in his saddle, waiting.

"*Gracias, mi hermana*," Señorita Revenge said. "He'll do nicely."

Longarm scowled and pitched his voice in a growl. "For what?"

Both señoritas smiled at him. He'd never minded two such beautiful women smiling at him, but he was minding these two very much. "You'll see," Valencia said.

The soft-bellied Kiowa returned presently, leading six mustang ponies. Longarm watched as the señorita and her ragged gang of warriors mounted up. The señorita rode off up the canyon, and Longarm turned to Valencia, still sitting on her palomino beside him.

"Where we goin'?"

"I told you—to my sister's lair."

"You're the queen of double-crossing bitches if I've ever seen one."

"Because I have decided to join up with my sister? I've had enough of the Quines. They provided me with food and clothing, but now it is time to go my own way. My sister's way."

"What way is that? To die fighting?"

She reached over and slapped the grullo's left hip, and as the horse and Longarm started up the canyon behind Señorita Revenge, Valencia, or Melah-ni, fell in behind him. Her voice echoed around the close stone walls, as did the clomps of her, Longarm's, and the following warriors' horses.

She said, "Why the hell not?"

And that was all she said until they rode out of the other end of the canyon and into a broad bowl filled with cool, purple shadows. The ground sloped away from the canyon.

Among the strewn rocks and cactus and scraggly pines and cedars, about a hundred yards away, hunched what appeared to be buildings that formed what remained of the main street of a town. An abandoned town. As Longarm rode toward it, beside Melah-ni and behind her sister, he could see the dilapidated condition of the scattered wooden structures. From what he could tell, there was no one here. The only sounds were the clomps of the horses around him, the chittering of birds, and the faint squawk of a chain likely suspending an ancient shingle over a boardwalk.

Where were Major Colby and Clara?

Dead?

"I'm missin' a coupla friends . . ." he said as they approached the buildings.

"Oh, the major and his daughter are friends of yours?" Señorita Revenge glanced over her shoulder at Longarm and shook her head. "You don't choose your friends very carefully, do you?"

"The girl had nothing to do with what happened to you, señorita."

"No, but her father did. Don't worry, Marshal Long. Er . . . Longarm. They are so far alive. Not very comfortable perhaps, but alive . . ."

They turned down what had once been the main street of a town that had obviously died soon after it had been started—likely before the war, judging by the rundown condition of the seven or eight frame or adobe brick buildings. In fact, there was only the one street, littered with tumbleweeds and grown up with cactus. There were five buildings on the street's left side and six on the right, all separated by gaps of rocks and weeds.

The last of the dying sunlight showed several caved-in roofs, boarded up windows—the boards badly sun-silvered—and outside stairs climbing to second or third stories but missing steps and railings. There were a couple

of saloons and a mercantile and a barbershop and what
Longarm assumed was a hotel, though the sign over its
front gallery was badly faded. He thought he could make
out the vague outline of an ace of spades.

As he rode past, a coyote leaped out the broken front
window onto the porch, looked at the procession clomping
by in the street, leaped over the rail at the end of the gallery, and disappeared into the desert twilight.

"Who's there?" a man's voice called thinly. "Who's
there? Please . . . help. . . . me . . . !"

Longarm turned to the right side of the street, where
there stood what appeared to be an old stone jailhouse,
judging by the stout front door with a small, barred window in it.

A large rock sat in the street in front of the door. There
was movement in the door's barred window, and Clara
Colby's voice called, "Is someone there? Oh, please help
us! Please! We've been captured by . . . !"

Clara let her voice trail off beneath the wicked, raucous
laughter of Señorita Revenge, who reined her horse to a
stop and threw her head back on her shoulders. Longarm
heard Clara sob and press her forehead against the bars.

"Christ!" He threw his left leg over the saddle horn and
hit the ground with a grunt, his injured calf squawking.
His hands cuffed in front of him, he walked toward the
jailhouse that was about the size of two regular cells. There
was a depression before the door, and in front of the
depression was the rock.

The rock moved. Longarm stopped.

It wasn't a rock. It was Major Colby's head. Señorita
Revenge had buried the man up to his neck in the street in
front of the jailhouse, where his daughter had a good view
of him.

"Longarm?" the major said, rocking his head from side

to side. "Oh, for chrissakes, Longarm . . . she's crazy. Absolutely *nuts!*"

The crude tattoo freshly carved into the man's forehead leaked dark red blood. The blood streaked his cheeks and dribbled over his jaws to continue on down his neck and into the dirt he was buried in.

Señorita Revenge laughed again. So did the warriors and Valencia, though Sam Quine's adopted daughter didn't laugh with as much vehemence as her sister this time.

"Longarm!" Clara called through the bars. She sobbed. "Isn't there something you can do? My father will die soon if he isn't dug up from fhere!"

"He will not die for a while," said Señorita Revenge, leaping down from her mustang's back. "Oh, no, I intend to keep the major alive at least until tomorrow."

She grabbed her bladder flask canteen from her horse and dropped to her knees beside Colby. "Open wide, Major, you murdering bastard."

She chuckled as she poured water over Colby's face. The major opened his mouth to catch as much of the streaming liquid as he could, squeezing his eyes closed, lapping at the water like a dog. It washed some of the blood from his face, only smeared the rest.

The warrior princess pinched the man's nose closed and wagged his head. "I am going to keep you alive until tomorrow, so that you will feel the pain of that Satan's mark all through the chilly desert night . . . unless a wolf rips your head off, that is!" She dropped the canteen, loosened a leather knot, and opened her vest, leaning forward to give Colby a good look at her naked breasts. "See that, Major? Have one more look at the mark you have on your head. But don't you dare ogle my tits, you bastard!"

She laughed and slapped Colby's face with the back of her hand.

Clara screamed.

Señorita Revenge said, "I'm going to give you another one just like it, on your chest, like mine, but not till the night has passed. You have all night to think about it. How do you like that?" She laughed again—shrill and devilish. It sounded like the call of she-coyote in heat.

"Longarm!" Clara screamed.

The lawman turned to Señorita Revenge. "Let the girl go. Her father's a murdering bastard. I understand that. But you've got no reason to put his daughter through this."

"Really?" The señorita gave him another of her insolent, jeering looks, jutting one hip and planting a fist on it. "What do you say we go into the hotel there, have a drink in the lovely saloon, and discuss it?"

"Me, too." Melah-ni dismounted and turned to Longarm and her sister, looking a little nonplussed, the lawman thought. "I will have a drink, as well, *mi hermana*. After all, I brought him here, did I not?"

"Of course, *mi hermana*," Señorita Revenge said, smiling placatingly. "I meant all three of us. He is both of ours, after all, isn't he?" She kissed her sister on the lips.

The soft-bellied Kiowa leaped down from his mustang, shaking his first at Señorita Revenge and yelling in their guttural tongue. She cowed him with a look. Straightening, he closed his mouth and glowered at Longarm, who returned the man's jealous, murderous look with a shrug.

He looked at Clara, who pressed her head against the bars in the jailhouse door, sobbing. He turned his gaze to the hotel on the opposite side of the street. He had no idea what there was to discuss. But what else was he going to do? His hands were cuffed.

"All right. Yeah, I could use a drink."

He wasn't lying.

Chapter 19

The two women flanking him, Señorita Revenge armed with his rifle and pistol, Longarm mounted the gallery steps of the old, dilapidated hotel, which, if it had ever been painted, was badly in need of a fresh coat. It also needed some new boards to replace the ones missing from the steps and the porch proper. The left side rail had fallen away to rot in the dust alongside the steps.

The hotel's heavy oak front doors were still standing, though the glass had long since been broken out of them. It crunched beneath Longarm's boots as he mounted the gallery. He heard a grunt behind him and stopped to stare over his shoulder at the soft-bellied Kiowa, who stood with one foot on a stock trough on the other side of the street, staring owlishly back at the lawman.

For the past couple of minutes, Longarm had been grooming an idea. It was only half-formed in his mind, but it buoyed his mood somewhat—at least gave him hope for himself and Clara Colby—and he found himself now grinning back at the angry Kiowa. Lifting both his cuffed hands, he pinched his hat brim to the man in mock salute.

Señorita Revenge gave him a shove, and he stumbled on through the doors and into the saloon's musty, shadowy drinking hall. "Don't pay attention to Rah," she said. "He's old and dried up. Can't even keep his cock hard for me anymore. It's like an old potato."

Melah-ni snickered at that, apparently still growing familiar with her sister's ribald chatter that sharply contrasted with her own upbringing among the Quines. Señorita Revenge must have enjoyed playing to her sister's audience. Swinging around, she yelled through the open door, "Did you hear that, Rah—you're like fucking a dead man. Go curl up with your bottle in the stable tonight, old man!"

Rah showed his teeth as the Kiowa warrior princess closed the door on him, then waved to him mockingly through the broken window.

Longarm quelled a laugh of his own. Hope rose in him as he continued to half-consciously formulate a plan. He looked around at the ruined room, only a few sticks of furniture remaining among the shadows and dirt. There was a bar on the room's right side, and it was coated in about three inches of dust and grit, cobwebs hanging from a wooden chandelier like netting over it and down its sides clear to the floor.

There was a wooden bucket on top of it, with a rusty tin ladle resting atop its cover. A rusty hurricane lantern stood beside the bucket. Señorita Revenge walked over, set Longarm's rifle across the bar, lit the lantern, and then removed the cover from the bucket. She shoved the ladle inside and sloshed it around, looking back at Longarm.

"Come over here and have a drink on Señorita Revenge," she said, hissing through her teeth. "I love that name! *Hermana de la Venganza*. It sounds even better in Spanish."

Longarm walked over and took the ladle out of her

hand. He sniffed the contents. It smelled weakly of grapefruit laced with hot peppers. He sipped. The pulque
grabbed at his throat and burned going down.

"Your home brew?" he asked.

"I know an old lady who makes it. I keep it here, where
I can have a drink now and then by myself. My Kiowa broth-
ers are barred from here. They are pigs. I drink here and
sleep here, and make them sleep in the barn. When I want
to fuck, I choose one and we do it outside like the dogs."

Melah-ni snickered, then reached out to take the ladle
from Longarm. "I want some."

"Be careful, my sister," said Señorita Revenge. "That
stuff is for women only." She jutted out her pointed tits
and rose up on the balls of her moccasins, regarding Longarm coolly. "Women and men."

"You forget—we're twins, Koma. The same age. I am
every bit as much woman as you." She looked smokily up
at Longarm from beneath her brows, then sipped the pulque. She choked and lowered her chin and pressed her fist
to her chest, but she held it down, and glanced at Señorita
Revenge with mild defiance. "See?"

The señorita took the ladle from her sister and polished
off the pulque as though she were drinking nothing stronger than water. She sighed and ran the back of her hand
across her mouth.

"So, señorita," Longarm said. "Tell me what it is we
have to discuss. I don't mean to rush, but it is getting late,
and I wouldn't want to stay out past my bedtime."

Señorita Revenge dropped the ladle back into the bucket
and walked around behind the bar. She stomped a few
times on the floor back there and then crouched down out
of sight. Longarm heard her grunting. There was a wooden
thud, as though she'd pried a board up out of the floor, and
then she straightened, her brown cheeks flushed from

exertion. She looked around carefully to see if anyone was near, and then she set a small, burlap-wrapped bundle atop the bar.

She hooked her finger at Longarm and Melah-ni. "Come closer. I don't want anyone outside to see this. This is for our eyes only."

She unwrapped the folds of burlap. A fist-sized chunk of gold sat glistening brightly in the light from the guttering lantern. It looked like a small sun that had been torn out of solid rock. Jagged-edged and smooth at the same time.

Longarm's lower jaw sagged in genuine shock at such a sight. He felt a wheezing breath flutter across his vocal cords as he tried to find his voice. To his right, Melah-ni also drew a ragged breath, and placed both her fine hands at the edge of the bar, pressing her fingertips into the ancient, begrimed wood.

"Where in hell did you find that?" Longarm asked, his heart thudding slowly but heavily.

"I will not only tell you but show you where it came from and where there are probably many more just like it . . . if you agree to become a partner with me and *mi hermana* in our business venture."

"A mine?" Longarm figured the town must have grown up around one. After all, this wasn't exactly mining country. But since the town was dead, wasn't the mine a bust?

"Sí." Senorita Revenge picked up the nugget and tossed it in her hand. "I found this when I walked off to relieve myself one night. The moon was shining on it. Floodwater from a rainstorm washed out the bank, exposing it. The fools who started this town quit too soon, it would seem."

Longarm stared at the rock. He didn't have to feign interest in it. He only had to hope that Señorita Revenge and Melah-ni believed he was so taken with it that he'd genuinely throw in with them in their business venture.

"What about Rah and the others?" he wanted to know, keeping his eyes on the gold.

"They don't know. There is no need for them to know. I have no use for them now. Tomorrow, after I have finished torturing that devil out there, I intend to shoot Rah and the others. You can help. And the gold will be ours . . ." She reached her free hand across the bar and raked her fingers lightly up from Longarm's thick neck to his chin. "Yours, mine, and Melah-ni's."

"Why me?"

"Because, you are a white man." Señorita Revenge slid her eyes to the front windows, dark now with the thickening night. "They are savages. I am ready for my sister's life of comfort, and you look like just the kind of man such a woman needs to make it especially comfortable."

"I found him first, *mi hermana*." Melah-ni stepped up close beside Longarm, snaked her arm around his back.

Ignoring her sister, Señorita Revenge kept her eyes on Longarm. "And you can help me shoot my savage friends and build a mine. Stake a claim. Do all that. Make it legal. And when we have all the gold we need, we can run away together to the ocean."

"*Mi hermana* . . ." Melah-ni started in a warning tone.

"Girls, girls," Longarm said, grinning at both of them. "There's enough of me to go around."

Melah-ni looked up at him towering over her and then smiled at her sister, flushing as she said, "He's right about that."

Señorita Revenge cackled devilishly. She held her probing, slightly rapacious gaze on Longarm. "What about your badge, lawman?"

Longarm looked at the gold in her hand, drew another ragged sigh, and shook his head. "What badge, señorita?"

"Can I trust you?"

Longarm held his cuffed hands across the bar and looked down at her breasts pushing out her vest. "Why don't you free my hands, so I can show you just how far you can trust me?"

Señorita Revenge studied him through slitted eyes. Her gaze slid across his broad chest and his stout arms straining the seams of his brown frock coat. She swallowed like a hungry cat and glanced at Melah-ni. "Free him, *mi hermana*. Maybe it is time to toast our partnership, and see just what kind of man I am getting."

"What kind of man *we* are getting, *mi hermana*," Melah-ni said, envy rising in her voice once more.

Señorita Revenge grabbed Longarm's Winchester off the bar and, holding it with one hand, rested it on her shoulder. "*Sí, sí* . . . 'we.'"

Melah-ni stuck her hand into her pocket and produced the handcuff key. Longarm lowered his hands, and she turned the key in the lock. When the cuffs opened, he removed them, wincing at the sudden flow of blood into the aching appendages, and dropped them into his pocket.

There was a loud, metallic ratcheting sound, and he looked across the grimy bar to see that Señorita Revenge had lowered the nugget to the bartop and was now aiming his cocked rifle at his heart. "Let me assure you, lover, what will happen if you try to pull a white man's trick."

He looked at the gun, her barely concealed breasts behind it. "Wouldn't think of it."

"You will room with me upstairs." Señorita Revenge slid the rifle toward the stairs rising at the back of the ruined saloon. She glanced at her sister, who stood glowering like a shopkeeper who'd just been told he'd given an unlimited amount of credit to a bankrupt customer.

Señorita Revenge smiled. And then Melah-ni offered a slow, lusty smile of her own.

The señorita walked over to her, and they kissed on the mouth again.

Outside, a scuffing sound rose on the gallery. Longarm looked past the girls to see a shadow move beyond the broken windows. Inwardly, he, too, smiled, and then Señorita Revenge took her sister's hand, and they walked together to Longarm. Señorita Revenge took his hand, as well.

"Hold on," he said, and then grabbed the handle of the pulque bucket. "Can't forget the toast, now, can we?"

Señorita Revenge gave the lantern to Melah-ni, and she followed Longarm and Melah-ni up the stairs. She remained a few steps behind them, so Longarm couldn't turn and grab the gun from her, and kept the rifle aimed at his back.

Naked, the only way you could tell the twins apart was of course the scar on the chest of Señorita Revenge, above the pointed, brown breasts that were exact replicas of her sister's. When they'd undressed each other—Melah-ni groaning sensually while her sister nuzzled her neck and kissed her lips very gently, tenderly—they undressed Longarm.

Naked, he sat back on the brass bed that, with a single dresser and a chair, was the room's only remaining furniture. He could feel the night chill through gaps in the walls. The light from the lantern played across the girls' tawny skin, twinkled in their dark eyes, and reflected beguilingly off the gold nugget on the dresser.

Señorita Revenge sat on one side of the bed, next to Longarm, and Melah-ni sat on the other. They leaned across his waist and pressed their lips together. He could hear the wet sounds of their kissing. Pulling away, Señorita Revenge looked down at his stone-hard cock, which angled up over his belly button, and gave a shudder, as though chilled by the night air.

She cursed very softly in what Longarm took to be Kiowa, and then she lowered her head to his belly and closed her mouth around the head of his cock. He felt her warm tongue caress him, the lips sucking at him gently at first and then hungrily. She groaned and stroked his balls.

Melah-ni said, "I told you it was big, *mi hermana*."

Señorita Revenge straightened her back and looked down at it, her lips parted, the lovely breasts below the grisly scar rising and falling heavily. She took Longarm's cock in her hand and pumped him several times. She had started to lower her head over the shaft again, when Melah-ni pushed her away gently and said, "It is my turn."

Melah-ni sucked his cock for several minutes while her sister kissed him and ladled up pulque for them all, each taking a sip. Outside, Longarm could hear only the silence of a held breath. Menacing.

Rah was lurking. He had to be. Still, Longarm pressed back the tension while the two girls took turns sucking his cock and kissing him and occasionally each other, and also sharing the pulque and generally learning to share everything.

He had to wait, bide his time, keep the girls busy until they were drunk enough to fall asleep. He just hoped that happened before Rah showed himself.

After a time, his nerves on edge despite the Kiowa liquor, the girls' ministrations keeping him hard, Longarm laid Señorita Revenge back on the bed's sparse covering of ragged blankets and looked at Melah-ni, who pooched her lips out indignantly.

"I'm gonna take your sister first," he said, and then lowered his head to suck each of her nipples in turn. "After all, it's her gold."

Señorita Revenge lay mewling and writhing, spreading her legs like a demented wildcat.

"*Sí*," said Melah-ni, breathing hard, nodding, the wings of her black hair hiding her face.

She hovered over Longarm, kissing him, while he fucked her sister. Señorita Revenge screamed and groaned and panted, and clawed at them both. When he brought her to satisfaction, she howled and yipped like a moon-struck coyote.

Then they all had another couple rounds of pulque.

Chapter 20

The girls danced drunkenly together in the lantern light. Melah-ni had lost all her inhibitions now, and she and her sister coupled like wildcats on the floor. Another hour passed as though in a dream, and then Longarm found both girls on him again, sucking his hard cock, before Melah-ni mounted him and hammered up and down on him, screeching.

Finally, silence. Longarm looked up at the ceiling with the light of the lantern flickering across it. His arms were pinned against the bed, each with a girl's warm, supple body on it. He lifted his head, listening.

Silence.

But Rah was out there. He had to be. He was too proud a warrior to let his woman go without a contest. Earlier, Longarm had seen the warrior's shadow outside the window downstairs. He was only waiting, biding his time, hoping to find his victims asleep before waking them with a knife's hot slashes.

Slowly, Longarm pulled each arm in turn out from beneath the girls. Just as slowly, he rose and found his

handcuffs. He closed one of the cuffs very quietly around
Señorita Revenge's wrist. And then very quietly he closed
the other cuff around a wrist of Melah-ni's. The girls slept
on, grunting, tossing their heads in their sleep.

Longarm grabbed his rifle. Naked, he stole to the door.
Pressing his head close to it, he listened.

Silence.

He could only hear the girls snoring and grunting in
the darkness of the bed and the breathy guttering of the
lantern. Carefully, quietly, he turned the doorknob.

The rusty bolt clicked. He drew the door open slowly.
The lantern light seeped out around him, illuminating the
wall on the other side of the hall and its cracked and rot-
ting wainscoting beneath faded wallpaper that hung in
tattered curls.

He stepped out. The ancient floorboards were gritty
beneath his bare feet. Squeezing the rifle in both hands,
he quietly levered a round into the chamber and looked
both ways down the hall. The lantern cast more shadows
than light out here.

He walked toward the stairs. As he did, a floorboard
squawked behind him. He smelled rancid grease, buckskin, and man sweat, felt the heat of a man behind him.

Rah gave a guttural war cry. Longarm's heart lurched
to life as he swung around to see the man outlined in front
of the open bedroom door, thrusting a blade toward the
lawman's belly. Not having time to fire, Longarm jerked
up the stock. The knife smashed against it. He jerked the
stock up again, slamming it hard against the underside of
Rah's chin. The man's jaws clacked together, and he gave
another scream as blood oozed between his lips.

Longarm was about to aim the Winchester's trigger,
but for some reason he was not sure of, something told him
to hit the floor, which he did, on his belly. Just in time.

Through the air not two feet above him rose the shrill song of a half dozen arrows. Longarm glanced up to see the wooden missiles catching the light from the room door an eyeblink before Rah's broad chest and bulging belly stopped them all.

Phittt! Phittt! Phittt!

With crunching thumps, they hammered the aging warrior's body, causing his eyes to nearly pop out of their sockets as he stumbled back, jerking as though he'd been lightning-struck. He screamed shrilly while grunts of surprise rose down the dark hall behind Longarm, who twisted around quickly, turning the rifle, and saw a half dozen figures crouching near the top of the stairs.

The shadows were reaching behind themselves to pluck more arrows from their quivers.

Longarm cut loose with the Winchester, gritting his teeth and racking and levering, racking and levering, the explosions sounding like kegs of detonated dynamite in the close confines. Through the wafting gray powder smoke, he saw one of the shadows hurl itself sideways. It disappeared down the stairs, howling.

Longarm heaved himself to his feet and, slipping on his own ejected shell casings, ran forward, leaping the writhing bodies of the dying warriors and dashing down the stairs. He'd taken five double steps when he stopped to see the Indian running toward the door. Vaguely, behind and above him he heard the enraged screams of Señorita Revenge. Keeping the brunt of his attention on the fleeing Kiowa, he aimed and fired.

The warrior screamed, dropped, and rolled up against the door, shaking.

"Noooooo!"

Longarm turned to see Señorita Revenge running along the balcony above and behind him, half-dragging Melah-ni.

The warrior princess screamed again as she approached
the top of the stairs, aiming Longarm's own Colt at him,
her eyes as wide as saucers, as black as the night but spitting fire.

The .44 leaped and roared in her hand. The bullet
plowed into the stair rail to Longarm's left.

Bringing the Winchester up quickly, he fired twice, both
bullets punching through the savage girl's breast and
throwing her back against the wall. Melah-ni was pulled
against the wall with her, and they both fell in a heap at
its base.

Señorita Revenge lay still, legs spread, head twisted at
an odd angle, her free hand thrown wide to one side.
Melah-ni lay beside her, sobbing, eyes wide in shock as she
gazed in horror at the two holes in her sister's chest—one
through the center of the grisly scar above her cleavage.

The next day around noon Longarm watched through his
field glasses as seven riders pulled a cloud toward him
across the rocky desert. He knelt on the lip of a sandstone
dike and kept one hand on the Winchester standing straight
up beside him, the other on the glasses.

Slowly, he released the tension in his hand. The riders
were within a hundred yards and pounding hard from the
west. On the still, oven-hot air he could hear them talking
beneath the thuds of their horses' hooves. The lead rider
was familiar—a tall, straight-backed man wearing a blue,
bib-front shirt, suspenders, and a ten-gallon hat. He, like
the others, wore a bandanna over his mouth and nose,
against the powdery dust.

When the riders were fifty yards away, Longarm lowered the field glasses. The riders were slowing, all seven
staring toward him. The six behind the lead rider were a
mix of Anglos and Mexicans. Slowly, Longarm stood,

raised the Winchester high above his head, and waved it broadly.

The riders continued until they'd stopped a few yards away, below his perch on the dike, and Sam Quine lowered his dusty red bandanna and stared up at him. The man's gingery-gray brows were dust-caked. He blinked and poked his hat brim back off his floury white forehead.

"What're you doing out here?"

"Huntin'."

"Me, too." Quine's long face was drawn, his eyes worried. "I'm looking for my daughter, Valencia. She rode off the ranch and didn't come back. I've been out here since yesterday. I'm worried Marquez got her."

Longarm turned his head to the right. Quine frowned, then touched spurs to his stallion's flanks and galloped off around the bulge in the dike, following the old Kiowa trail he and his riders had taken to get here and which Longarm had been following back toward San Simon. Quine's riders regarded Longarm owlishly from over their dusty neckerchiefs, squinting against the clay-colored dust, and booted their horses after their boss.

Longarm turned and walked down the sloping backside of the dike. Quine and his men appeared on his left, heading toward the shaded nest in the boulders where Major Colby, Clara, and Valencia all sat on the ground, the Colbys leaning back against one rock together, Valencia against the other, nearest her adoptive father riding toward her. The horses were picketed back in the rocks aways, near a runoff spring.

Valencia looked as haggard as the Colbys, her pretty clothes dusty and bedraggled, her hair hanging in her eyes. Colby sat staring straight out into space, the way he'd been staring since Longarm had dug him from the ghost town's street fronting the old jail. They'd been on the trail for over

a day, riding slowly, taking their time, and he hadn't said
a word or even given the impression that he knew what
Longarm or his daughter said to him.

A blood-spotted white bandage was wrapped around
the top of his head, covering the savage tattoo.

Clara sat beside him, holding his hand, looking tired
and worried and sunburned—still in shock from her travail
but holding up better than Longarm would have thought
her capable.

Quine's men reined up before his daughter. "Valencia!"
As his men checked their own horses down several yards
behind him, Quine leaped out of his saddle and dropped
to a knee beside his daughter, who suddenly looked hor-
rified. Quine didn't seem to notice. "Good Lord—I've been
looking all over for you, girl!"

He held her tightly. Valencia kept her back stiff, looking over her father's shoulder at Longarm, frightened and
befuddled.

Quine pulled away, his gloved hands squeezing her
arms. "What happened?"

She only stared at Longarm, seemingly as unable to
speak as Major Colby, who continued to stare straight off
into space, the bloody, white bandanna glowing brightly
in the midday sun. Clara looked from the Quines to Longarm and back again.

Longarm stopped near Quine's fine roan stallion and
shouldered his rifle. He looked at the adopted Kiowa girl
and then at her father, and sighed heavily. "Lost her way
for a while, Mr. Quine. That's all. Best take her on home."

"Where did you find her?" Quine asked.

Longarm hiked a shoulder. "Does it really matter?"

"I thought for sure either Marquez or Señorita Revenge
got her."

Valencia looked at Longarm. He held her gaze for a few

seconds. "I don't know about Marquez, but Señorita Revenge is dead. So is her gang. She won't be terrorizing this country anymore."

Quine looked at Colby. "What happened to him?"

"He was her last victim. Like I said, she won't be terrorizing this country anymore. Take your daughter home, Mr. Quine. I'm sure she could use a good hot bath and a cool bed."

Quine stood, taking Valencia's hand. "Come on, daughter. Let's get you home."

Longarm retrieved her horse, tightened the latigo strap, and slipped the bit back between its teeth. Quine helped Valencia into the saddle. She stared down at Longarm, tears dribbling down her cheeks. "Thank you, Marshal."

Longarm gave her the reins and stepped back. Quine mounted up, and he and Valencia headed out ahead of the pack. The former Melah-ni glanced once more over her shoulder to squint through the group's roiling dust at Longarm.

When the dust had settled, Longarm turned to Clara and her father. Colby looked like a mere husk, a dead man with a heartbeat, albeit a weak one.

"Longarm, what will happen to my father after . . . the horrible thing he did . . . ?"

"I don't know, Clara. I really don't. I'll have to take him back to Denver with me. We'll see what a federal judge says. I reckon he'll see a doctor or two, see if they can get his mind back."

She looked at the shell of her father sitting beside her, staring at the sun-blasted slope of the dike opposite the shaded boulder nest. Tears filled her eyes. "He's a bad man, but I can't help still loving him." She sobbed and looked at Longarm. "Oh, whatever will become of *me?*"

Longarm offered a reassuring smile. "Clara, I got a

feelin' you're a lot stronger than you think you are. I'll take you to Denver with me. I know some people there who will be proud as punch to help a young lady in need."

He was thinking of the family of General Larimer, including his lovely niece, Cynthia.

"They . . . and I . . . will see you standin' on your own two feet in no time. You'll like Denver." Longarm gave her a wink. "Lots of handsome young men there."

"And you're there—right, Custis?"

"Oh, I'm there, too—when I ain't workin', that is, which I am most of the time."

"You won't take me there and forget about me—will you, Custis? I'm very scared!"

"Oh, don't you worry, Miss Clara. I could never forget about you." Remembering their time in the springs behind the major's headquarters, he wasn't lying.

He walked back to where he'd hobbled their mounts. "I'll fetch our horses. It's time we rattled our hocks to the east. In a few more hours we should be back in San Simon."

They mounted up and rode off. Longarm looked back in the direction of the ghost town that lay on the other side of the sun-blasted Chisos Range.

Señorita Revenge.

He'd never forget her, either.

Watch for

**LONGARM AND
THE TOWN FULL OF TROUBLE**

the 416th novel in the exciting LONGARM
series from Jove

Coming in July!

LONGARM

GIANT-SIZED ADVENTURE FROM AVENGING ANGEL LONGARM.

BY TABOR EVANS

penguin.com/actionwesterns

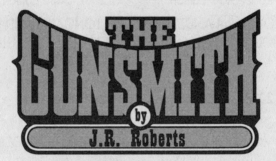